DARK AMBITIONS

A CLASS 5 NOVELLA

MICHELLE DIENER

ABOUT DARK AMBITIONS

Rose McKenzie is adapting to life with the Grih, and now that the threat of war with the Tecran is over, she's hoping to settle into what passes for a normal life far from Earth and everything she knows. When she gets the chance to join an exploration team who are going down to collect information from a planet in Grihan airspace, she jumps at the chance to stretch her legs and breath some real air.

But unknown to the Grih, someone is already on the planet, and they don't want anyone to know what they're up to. They ambush the exploration team and take them prisoner, but they don't realize they didn't get everyone. They didn't get Rose.

With her partner, Dav, and his spaceship the *Barrist* lured away by a distress signal, Rose and Sazo, along with a furry friend Rose has made, are the exploration team's only hope of rescue.

Note: DARK AMBITIONS is a novella set in the Class 5 series and occurs after the events in DARK MATTERS, book 4 in the series.

CHAPTER 1

"I WANT you to stay with Sazo." Dav threaded his fingers through Rose's hair and massaged her scalp with clever fingers.

She gave a hum of contentment. "No."

"No?" His fingers stilled and he tilted his head to look down at her.

"No. There's a beautiful planet below. A large group of your crew is going down to it, and I want to go with them."

"I just don't like the idea of you down there without me." He gave her a look with earnest eyes, and she decided he must have gotten away with something when he looked at her like that some time in the past, and was trying it out again.

"I need the wind on my face," she told him simply. "I want to breath actual air."

He sighed and his hands slid down to her shoulders and rubbed. "I know, but this distress call from the asteroid mining station can't be ignored, and I really don't like to be without you. Staying with Sazo is the safest option."

"There'll be five exploration crew and eight soldiers with me. And Sazo, hovering right overhead." She had to draw a line in the sand. There was no concrete threat to her below, and she wouldn't be excluded from something she truly wanted to do, just in case.

The small shuttle they were traveling on from Sazo's Class 5 battleship slid through the gel wall onto the flight deck of the *Barrist* and Dav stepped back, his hands lingering on her shoulders. "I worry."

"I do, too." She tilted her head. "You're the one going to a known trouble spot."

He watched her for a beat and then gave a quick nod. "Be careful, then."

She pulled him close to her and went up on her toes to kiss him. "I promise."

The shuttle landed, and the ramp began to lower.

Dav kissed her back, a hard, possessive claiming of her mouth, and then strode to the open door and scooped up the bag she'd brought for her trip as he exited.

She followed him down the ramp.

He was talking in quiet, serious tones to Jia Appal, his second-in-command and the person leading the soldiers standing ready to go down to the planet below, by the time she reached the bottom.

Jia looked up, over Dav's shoulder, and grinned at her as Dav handed her Rose's bag, and Rose grinned back.

Dav said something, and Jia became serious, and whatever she said back to him must have been enough, because he gave a nod, blew a kiss to Rose, and jogged off toward the bridge.

"Ready to go?" Jia asked.

The explorer's ramp was down, the sleek shuttle's engines were on. Rose could see the head explorations officer, Lieutenant Kila, directing the last of her equipment into the hold.

Rose took her own bag from Jia and gave a nod. Excitement bubbled up inside her. It had been so long since she'd walked on actual ground and breathed fresh air.

She followed Jia into the shuttle and sat beside her on one of the comfortable seats inside.

"What was Dav saying to you? Protect the little woman at all costs?"

Jia laughed. "Something like that."

"There isn't any real need to be concerned is there?" Rose twisted slightly to grab the harness straps and clip herself in.

"No. There are predators on Vuyn, but we have sound disruptors we can use to keep them away, and the plant life isn't poisonous to us, according to Kila. The planet seems quite similar to Calianthra, actually. Very tall trees, lots of fern-like plants on the forest floor, and a mild summer temperature. It could well be a place for the Grih to expand, as there aren't any higher level sentients that we can find. Vuyn's been mapped and recorded as livable, but we've had a non-interference order on it up until now. Kila needs to make sure there hasn't been any changes down there before we can put the planet on the cleared-for-settlement list."

"It's very green." While Jia had been speaking, the explorer had launched, and was headed down toward Vuyn. It lay below them, green and silver in the sunlight, and Rose tapped her earpiece.

"You looking at the planet, Sazo?"

"I've been looking at it for hours." He sounded faintly amused.

"It's so beautiful. Not a lot of water, though, or is that on the other side?" She leaned against the transparent wall of the explorer for a better look.

"A lot of the water is covered in a green algae," Kila said from her seat. "That's why it looks like there's very little water. The silver areas you see are the few areas of water where the algae isn't growing. I don't know what keeps it in check in those places, but that will have to be a project for the second trip. This trip, we're in the forests, making sure there aren't any signs of higher sentience in any of the mammals."

There'd been no orange signatures from the scan Kila had done last year, Dav told her this morning. But evidently the scanner wasn't sophisticated enough to catch a species that was almost at higher sentient status. That was something Kila had to do herself, along with her team, and Rose was just happy she was allowed to come along.

"The *Barrist* has left," Sazo told her. "Time to its destination, five hours."

Rose looked back to where the *Barrist* had been, but it was really gone, gone. Disappeared. Off to check out a faint distress signal from the asteroid belt in the next solar system along from this one.

Sazo was still there, though. A big, black prickle ball hanging in space, looking menacing.

"Did Dav tell you to watch out for me, too?" Rose asked him.

"No." Sazo was a master at voice inflection, and she realized she'd insulted him. "I will always watch out for you, whether he asks me to or not."

She knew he could see her. He was in every visual comms feed, every system the *Barrist* and its shuttles had, and so she blew him a kiss. "Right back at you."

The soft snort she heard in her ear told her she had been forgiven.

And then she turned to look at the sea of green below and the promise of adventure. She was about to go outside!

CHAPTER 2

THE AIR WAS MOISTURE-LADEN—FILLED with the scent of dark, rich earth and growing things. It was early afternoon on Vuyn, and the sunlight was warm and golden.

Rose drew in a deep breath as she stepped off the runner, and did the bounce test.

She had denser bones and muscles than the Grih, and in some places, gravity didn't hold her down as much as it had on Earth.

This wasn't one of those places.

"The size and atmosphere of this planet is similar to Earth. It will be very much like being back there," Sazo said into her earpiece, and the thought of that made her suddenly tear up.

She swallowed hard, mortified at the swamp of emotions that overtook her.

"Ready to go, Rose?" Jia had been talking to her team, four armed men and three women besides herself, and they were standing together at a break in the treeline, waiting for everyone else.

Unable to speak around the tightness in her throat, Rose gave a nod and bent to pick up her pack.

Kila and her four colleagues were helping each other strap their packs to their backs. The decision had been made to go on foot and go as quietly as possible. No hover motors or engines to scare away wildlife. Their walking through the forest would be enough of a disturbance.

They were carrying everything they needed themselves.

Dara, one of Kila's underlings, and one of the first people Rose ever met when she first came aboard the *Barrist*, readjusted her straps and ambled over to where Rose was waiting.

"If that pack gets too heavy for you, let us know. We can always divide up what's inside between us."

Rose looked up at her, bemused. They always thought she was weaker, because she was shorter, but they forgot that she was stronger than they were for her size. She could have said something, but she realized she had gotten used to it. "Thanks, Dara. I'm fine for now."

"Everyone ready? Let's go." Kila sounded the happiest Rose had heard her in a while.

She tagged on the back of Kila's group and four of Jia's team waited until she had passed them, and then got into line.

It looked like Jia was bracketing them either end with security.

Dav would be happy.

She smiled, and hoped that everything was all right on the *Barrist*. It wasn't a battleship, it was an explorer, but it had defensive shields and weapons.

The distress call they were answering was from a small meteor mining station, which was located firmly in Grihan airspace, so the chances were the call was for help because of an accident of some kind, not that the station was under attack.

Hopefully, those days were gone now that the Tecran were under Council rule for five years, and the Garmman were being closely watched. The other three members of the council—the Grih, the Bukari, and the Fitali—had formed a tight-knit alliance within the alliance, and neither the Tecran nor the Garmman were strong enough to take them on.

She would talk to Jia later, when they took a break, and make sure Dav hadn't minimized the risks of going to give aid to the mining station, although if he had, there wasn't anything she could do about it down here on Vuyn.

She grinned suddenly at the reality of being here, really walking on the surface of a planet again, and then turned her face upward at the annoyed *bak bak bak* of a bird in the branch above her.

The trees were immense, stretching high into the sky, and she couldn't see anything through the thick foliage on the lower branches.

"It's like a road system up there," Dara said. She was just in front of Rose, and she'd stopped and turned to look up as well.

"Sounds fun." Rose eyed the lowest branch, but it was too high for her to reach. "You ever been up there?"

Dara shook her head. "All our information on Vuyn has so far been observations from probes we've sent down. This is the first time any of us have set foot down here."

No wonder Kila looked like all her Christmases had come at once. Rose looked around at the delicate curl of the ferns at the base of the trees and the width of the tree trunks, and hugged herself, she was so happy. It was like her Christmases had come at once, too.

She angled her face to feel the soft whisper of wind, and caught a beam of sunlight that had managed to poke a finger through the foliage.

The scrape of a boot on stone reminded her of the four soldiers behind her, waiting for her to keep moving, and she sent them an apologetic smile and sped up a little to close the gap between Dara and herself.

She missed Jay Xaltro and Vree Halim, the guards she'd had when she first arrived on the *Barrist*. They'd been attacked and injured while they were guarding her a few months ago, and both had ended up being assigned to lighter duties on other ships for a while. Dav said they wanted to come back, though, and she was looking forward to seeing them again.

The soldiers in Jia's team were familiar faces, but she didn't know any of them personally. She would probably know them all quite well by the time they were finished here.

She hoped so.

She could stand to make a few more friends.

They were scheduled to be here for a week, which was the longest she would have spent uninterrupted with a small group of Grih since she'd been dropped into this strange new reality. Sazo had agreed to allow the group to return to his Class 5 if the *Barrist* wasn't back by the time they were done, but Dav had been adamant the *Barrist* would be five days at most.

She didn't know if she and Dav had been apart for five days since they'd met.

She suddenly missed him with a sharp, throat-catching intensity, and tears swam in her eyes for the second time that day.

Wow. She really needed to pull herself together. Being on an actual planet again was obviously something she needed more badly than she realized.

She blinked back the moisture, annoyed with herself but still feeling weepy. Her breath hitched a little, and she rubbed her face with both hands, and then, because she wasn't looking where she was going, stumbled and almost tripped over a root as she walked.

"You all right?" The soldier behind her called out.

She waved a hand at him, refusing to turn around in case she looked like she had been blinking back tears, and felt a wave of embarrassed heat wash through her cheeks.

Ugh! She really needed to get it together.

She breathed in deeply, and let the constant rustle of leaves and the calls of the invisible birds overhead relax her. This was food for her soul.

They walked for nearly two hours over mostly flat ground, although they had to find ways around some clumps of extra thick foliage. They'd parked the explorer shuttle they'd come down in as close to the forest as they could, but Kila wanted to set up camp in a spot that was deep enough in the massive woods that they would be able to find the widest variety of species.

As she followed Dara into a sun-filled clearing, Rose saw Kila looking carefully around with hands on hips, and realized she was tired enough that she hoped the explorations officer would decide this was far enough.

She shouldn't be tired. She exercised daily in the gym, but the fresh air might be causing the sudden exhaustion that dragged at her.

She yawned.

Suddenly everyone put their packs down, and started pulling out tents, and she realized she must have zoned out while the decision was made that this was the spot.

She didn't care, she was just glad she could sit down in a bit.

She pulled her own tent out. "How does the tent work again?" she asked Sazo.

She didn't speak to him a lot when she was with the crew of the *Barrist*—it seemed to freak them out and she had the sense it was a little bit rude on her part to carry on a conversation they could only hear one side of—but no one was paying her any attention now, they were busy doing their own thing.

"You hold the blue tabs and flick it," he answered. "I can't see you, the forest is too dense. Are you setting up camp?"

"Yes, we had to make a few course adjustments because there were tangles we had to go around, but I can hear a stream nearby, and we have a really nice clearing. You might be able to see us if you zoom in because there is quite a lot of blue sky overhead."

"Got you." Sazo sounded pleased. "You're not as far in as I would have expected, but obviously the going wasn't as easy as Lieutenant Kila anticipated."

"Nor me." Rose's tone was wry. "I'm more out of shape than I thought. I've always known gym fitness isn't the same as outdoor fitness, but damn, I'm wiped out." She held the slim package that was apparently her tent by the blue tabs and flicked, and then let it go in surprise as it popped into a very decent sized sleeping quarters. Ha. She wasn't even going to have to rough it that much here. Not that she minded roughing it for the pleasure of being outdoors, but this was even better.

Around her, a little tent city had sprung up, and Jia caught her eye and walked over to her. "I'd prefer you to be in the middle of the camp, not on the edge here, if you don't mind."

"Sure." Rose didn't mind at all. And if it kept everyone happy, why not? She picked up one side of the tent, Jia picked up the other, and they placed it in the inner circle that was forming.

Rose then set about putting her pack and her sleeping mat and smooth, soft sleeping bag inside and sorting through the pre-made food at the bottom of her pack.

Since she'd been accepted into Grihan society, she'd had a lot of bad luck with food, but Sazo had made a point of finding things she liked to eat, and between them, they'd created a menu that she actually enjoyed eating.

The days of going hungry because absolutely nothing appealed to her were over, thank goodness.

They settled in as the sun sank down, with some of the group gathering up wood and creating a fire circle with small rocks and stones.

Rose went to help them, keeping close to the clearing as she foraged for sticks.

As she stepped over a very large branch beneath a giant tree, she heard a small, high-pitched squeaking on the ground. The gloom made it difficult for her to see what it was or exactly where it was coming from.

To her ear, it sounded distressed.

"Where are you?" she crooned, crouching down.

The branch looked like it had snapped off from the tree recently.

"What's going on?" Sazo asked.

"I can hear something squeaking. It sounds hurt or afraid." She shuffled along the length of the branch on her haunches. "Oh, wow." The little nest she found was an intricate weaving of thin sticks and long, tapering leaves, a fully enclosed oval with a small hole in the middle. "Are you in there?"

"You found it?" Sazo sounded a little worried. "Be careful. It could be dangerous."

"There's a nest. I think it's inside." She didn't know what to do. Was it better to not touch the nest?

The one side of the intricate structure was slightly crushed under the branch, and she carefully lifted the branch up and pulled it away.

A little face popped out, so cute, so tiny, she just blinked at it, and extended her hand.

The little creature extended two tiny limbs, grabbed onto her fingers, and then climbed up onto the back of her hand.

They stared at each other for a moment.

"I'm just going to check to see if you were alone in there." She slowly, gently, turned her hand, and the little ball of fluff scrabbled for purchase until it was sitting on her cupped palm. She lifted the nest, and the little baby started its distressed squeaking again.

Inside, she saw a bigger version of the baby, dead.

"Mama got killed, and you've been trapped in there with her." She put the nest down and stood, her hand out to look at the baby more carefully.

It wriggled on her palm, she could feel its little feet flexing, and then, suddenly, it jumped, stretching its arms and legs out wide as it leapt for her chest and hooked tiny claws into her shirt to hang on.

She managed to swallow her squeak of surprise. It was like a glider, or a tiny flying squirrel, with flaps of skin that flared as it jumped. A tiny, furry flying handkerchief.

She ran a tentative finger down its back, and it seemed to tuck in closer to her, so she cupped it with her hand, bent again to pick up the sticks she'd gathered, and made her way back to the camp.

"Looks like I've found an orphan," she told Sazo.

"Like me," he said.

She grinned as she thought of darkly menacing Sazo, and this tiny bundle of cuteness, having anything in common. "Yes, just like you."

CHAPTER 3

"I DON'T KNOW what it is," Kila said. She was trying to get a good look at the baby, but it kept turning its little face against Rose's shirt and shivering in fear.

"It looks a lot like something from Earth called a flying squirrel. Only much smaller." Rose soothed it, gently stroking it from head to tail, and it made a chirping sound. "It has to be hungry. What should we feed it?"

Kila shook her head. "Nothing, Rose. We don't interfere with the wildlife on this planet. If it can survive on its own, it will. You need to put it back where you found it."

Rose had half-expected this response. "I understand that, but its mother is dead. I can't put it back in that nest with a dead body." She tried to put the baby down on the ground, but it wouldn't let go of her shirt. She sighed and looked over at Kila. "I get your point, and I agree with it, but at the same time, I'm not going to hurt it, or force it to do something it doesn't want to do, and right now, it wants to hold onto me. I won't stop it going whenever it wants to, but in the meanwhile, it might be too weak to do anything else but cling to me. If we feed it something, that might help it leave when it's strong enough."

Kila looked at the baby again, the hard line of her mouth softening. She sighed. "All right. I don't know if it's been weaned yet. How big was the mother?"

Rose showed her with her hands, and Kila tilted her head from side to side as she thought about it.

"It might be weaned if the mother was that size in comparison to it. Look for small insects to feed it." She walked away, toward the fire that was starting to look like a really nice campfire.

Huh.

Rose narrowed her eyes as she watched Kila go. *You think I'm going to baulk at catching bugs.*

She gave a snort.

Kila thought wrong.

She moved after the explorations officer and crouched beside the pile of wood everyone had collected. The flames cast an orange glow over the sticks and branches, and she caught the gleam of a hard insect shell.

"How does this look?" she asked her orphan, holding the wriggling bug out to it.

It let out a strange, hissing squeak and grabbed at the bug. Tiny sharp teeth bit down on it, and Rose heard a delicate crunching sound.

She felt ridiculously pleased with herself.

"I fed the baby," she told Sazo.

"What did you feed it?"

"Some dark brown insect with a hard shell on its back." She looked around for another one, but the baby had fallen asleep on her palm, the bug completely consumed.

Time for her own dinner.

The Grih had taken seats around the fire, and Rose could see they were obviously enjoying the change from being inside the *Barrist* as much as she was. She went to fetch one of the meals she'd brought, found a place next to Dara, and put the baby glider next to her in a nest she'd made of one of her t-shirts.

"It's very sweet," Dara said, peering at it. "If it doesn't leave in the night, we can have a good look at it tomorrow."

Rose ate her food and listened to the others talking. She often felt an outsider when she was in a group of Grih, something she knew would change over time. She hadn't been part of their society for even half a year yet, and these things took time. Still, she sometimes found it hard when her main sources of contact were Dav and Sazo, and the occasional comm conversation with one of the three other Earth women who'd been taken at the same time as she had been.

The conversation fell into a natural lull. She tilted her head up to look at the sea of stars stretching above the high tops of the trees. When she looked back at the fire, its light flickered and glowed on the faces of the Grih around her. It reminded her of the camping holidays she'd taken as a child, the fun she'd had sitting around the fire.

She realized for the first time in a long time, she wanted to sing in public.

Usually, the Grihan reaction freaked her out, and she avoided it unless she was asked to sing in an official capacity. She didn't want them to expect her to sing on demand, so maybe she'd gone hard in the opposite direction.

She cleared her throat. "On Earth, when we go into the forest or the wilderness and build a fire like this, we often sing songs together. Would you like me to sing one?"

For a moment, there was absolute silence, just the crack and pop of the wood in the fire, and the rustle of the trees.

"I would." Dr. Hri Revil spoke up. She was the medic in the group, brought along in case anyone was injured, and she was one of the few people Rose counted as more than just an acquaintance on the *Barrist*. They ate meals together if they saw each other in the officers' mess, and they even worked out together at the gym.

"Any objections?"

There was suddenly a lot of head shaking.

She started by singing *She'll Be Coming Round the Mountain*. It was, in her mind, a quintessential campfire song, although she stopped after the second verse.

"She'll be wearing pink pajamas?" Sazo asked, bemused.

Rose gave a laugh as she sang the last *yipee yai*. "That's my favorite line."

She looked around at the absolute focus of the Grih. "Would you like another?"

"We would." Dara leaned a little closer to her.

She thought about it, and the memory of sitting around the fire at summer camp, singing *These Are a Few of My Favorite Things* from the movie *The Sound of Music* with her best friend Jenny Dawson washed over her. She hadn't thought of Jenny in years. She started to sing, a little hoarsely at first as the memory of it caught at her throat, but she warmed into it and managed to hold the last note satisfyingly well.

When she was done, there were a few soft ululations of appreciation, although they were subdued.

It was probably a combination of the Grih knowing she didn't like effusive praise for her singing, and the fact that they were on a strange planet, surrounded by soaring trees. It felt almost sacrilegious to make a loud noise.

She cleared her throat. "Thank you. This has brought back good memories for me."

"You can indulge your trip down memory lane anytime you want," Hri Revil said in a heartfelt voice, and a ripple of laughter ran around the group.

Warmth bloomed inside Rose that had nothing to do with the fire. It sometimes seemed to her that she would never make connections or friends like she had on Earth, but it *did* take time, she reminded herself. There was no rush. She had her whole life with the Grih ahead of her.

"I want to thank you also for asking me to join you on the expedition." She turned to Kila. "I needed to come down and breathe real air more than even I knew."

Kila paused awkwardly before she gave a nod. "We are happy to have you with us."

But that pause spoke volumes.

Kila hadn't asked her, Rose realized. Dav had most likely told her to include Rose. Before the distress signal came through and he realized he'd have to leave the team for a while to check it out, no doubt.

It was nepotism and unfair advantage and meddling on Dav's side, but Rose couldn't get cross about it. She was too happy to be here.

A sudden, debilitating weariness weighed her down, and she almost staggered to her feet. "I'm so tired. I'm going to turn in."

She exchanged good nights with them and scooped up the orphan, still fast asleep and curled up happily in its nest. It was an effort to even clean her teeth but she forced herself and then pulled on warm pyjamas and collapsed onto her bed.

She wondered about Dav, about how he was doing, and then sleep sucked her under.

CHAPTER 4

ROSE WOKE to the sound of birds chattering so loudly, they sounded like they were sitting around her tent.

Maybe they were.

She stretched, took a deep breath, and then remembered the baby.

She twisted on her side to look at where she'd put the t-shirt nest the night before, and found two big eyes looking at her. It saw she was awake and began to chirp enthusiastically.

"Hungry, sweetpea?" She sat up, yawned, and then used the wipes they'd all been given in place of a shower. They weren't the same as standing under hot water, which her muscles would have loved right now, but they were better than nothing. She wriggled into her clothes and put a hand out, and the baby scrambled up onto her palm. "Let's get something to eat."

As she stood, a wave of nausea rolled over her, and she had to bend at the waist, the hand with the baby glider out to the side as she breathed through it. After a moment, the feeling passed, and she slowly straightened.

Did she say something about this reaction, or keep it to herself?

She decided to play it straight, or she could see it being used against her in the future if there really was something wrong. She wanted nothing to be used as an excuse not to let her come down with the exploration team again.

"I'm not sure if something down here is affecting me, or if I ate something bad last night, but I nearly threw up," she told Sazo.

"Get Dr. Rivel to check you out." He was worried. "There shouldn't be anything down there that's dangerous to you, but we don't have all the information. That's why you're down there to begin with." He paused. "What is that noise?"

"Birds," she said, as she ducked down to get out of the tent. As soon as they were outside, the baby jumped onto her chest again, and clung on for dear life.

The camp was busy. It looked like she was the last to emerge, and most of the others were sitting around the fire, drinking grinabo and eating a quick meal.

She waved, moved off to the latrine Jia's soldiers had constructed the night before, and then made her way back to the fire.

"Here you go." Jia handed her a cup of grinabo, and she took it gratefully. The baby glider was still gnawing on the bug they'd found on the way back from the eco-toilet. Rose had found it by rolling over a fallen branch and letting the baby grab one of the insects that had tried to scatter for itself.

One of the soldiers, Wester, she thought his name was, walked past them with a steaming bowl, and as the scent of it wafted toward her, Rose felt her gorge rise, and she gagged.

"What is it?" Jia crouched beside her, and Rose shook her head as she breathed through it.

"I don't do well with some Grih dishes. Rost grain is one of them." She nodded in Wester's direction, and forced herself to take a sip of her grinabo. The nutty taste helped and she finally raised her head.

"I didn't realize your reaction was that bad." Jia looked at her sympathetically. "Can you eat korla?"

The slightly pink-tinged bread was Rose's favorite, and she

nodded and took the slice that Jia offered her. It was warm and freshly toasted.

The baby looked at it with big, bright eyes, but Rose was too scared to give it some in case it wasn't good for it.

"It's still here?" Kila asked, bringing over her grinabo and sitting beside them. She gently pulled the baby off Rose's shirt and held it firmly while she looked it over. "It's female, and it's probably omnivorous."

The baby blinked at her, and then bared its teeth and tried to twist in her hands.

Rose crooned to it, reaching to take it back, and it climbed with tiny, sharp claws up her chest and tucked itself against her skin beneath her neck.

She stroked it, and then looked up into Kila's accusing gaze.

"I know, I know. But I'm not going to be cruel to her, and she needs some cuddling."

"If we hadn't come along, she'd have died, and that would have been the natural cycle of life." Kila folded her arms.

"Yes. But we did come along. We inserted ourselves into this ecosystem, and I can't bring myself to simply abandon her. Not when that would now involve pulling her off me." She stroked the shivering little back gently, her fingertips brushing the soft, fluffy fur. "And I'm not going to do that, sweetpea."

"What is a *sweetpea*?" Dara asked. She'd come over to watch the standoff between her boss and Rose with an amused gleam in her eye, and now she crouched down in front of Rose to have another look at the baby glider.

The baby's tail twitched a bit as she got close, but she stayed still otherwise.

"It's a term of endearment on Earth. And the name of a pretty flower."

"Is that what you're going to call her?" Jia asked, and Kila made a hum of disapproval.

"Why not?" Rose cupped the little body with her hand, because it felt a little cool this morning, and stood. "What's the plan for today?"

"We'll do a simple observation, just walking with lenses clipped to everyone's shirts, and gather information until this afternoon. We can come back and look at the footage before it gets dark so we can decide what to focus on tomorrow." Kila bent to pick up her bowl and cup, and everyone sprang into action, following her lead.

They had had more of an audience than Rose realized.

She was often the focus of attention—not always friendly—but she hoped by the end of this trip that she wouldn't seem so strange to everyone.

She cleared up her own things, went to brush her teeth in her tent, and then put water, snacks and lunch into a small pack.

Sweetpea clung to her shirt and then climbed up to sit on her shoulder and Rose grinned when she felt a tiny clawed hand grab her hair for balance. She joined the others and they set off at an easy pace.

A few people murmured to each other in quiet conversation, but the sigh of the wind and the crunch of leaves underfoot muted that out. Rose soaked it up hungrily, enjoying the feel of the sun on her face where it managed to filter through the trees, and enjoying the cool gloom of the shade where it didn't.

When she saw a beetle or insect on the ground or a tree, she lifted Sweetpea off her shoulder and put her close to it.

She pounced three times, and managed to get one beetle out of it.

She was learning.

Kila saw what she was doing, and for a change gave a nod of approval. "You're teaching her to hunt for herself. That's good."

Rose knew the spike of annoyance she felt was really just because she didn't like how Kila made it sound as if she was giving her approval, when Rose wasn't doing it for Kila's approval at all.

Kila didn't mean to get up her nose, but she and the explorations officer had had a rocky relationship from the start. She needed to let it go.

She concentrated on getting back the calm she'd felt before.

The sound of water had been audible for about ten minutes, and they headed toward the source of it. The noise got louder and louder the closer they got and when Rose stepped into the clearing behind Dara she gasped at the cascade of water which tumbled and foamed over rocks and then swirled into a pool.

Dara moved to the edge of the water and lowered a probe into it, then took out a handheld and tapped away at it for a few minutes. "Nothing dangerous in there. Some fish and a few crustaceans, but that's all."

The clearing was large enough that the sun flooded it with light, and the water danced like diamonds. Rose crouched beside Dara and dipped her hand in.

It was warm on the top, cool below the surface.

"Can I swim?" she asked. No one looked surprised at her question, but then, she was the person onboard the *Barrist* who used the pool the most.

"I wouldn't mind someone diving in with a lens," Kila said.

Rose nodded, stripping out of her boots, socks and pants, but keeping her t-shirt and underwear on. Dara clipped a lens to her and Rose put Sweetpea, who had fallen asleep again after her beetle lunch, onto the pile of clothes.

She dived in, going right to the bottom, and sat cross-legged on the smooth pebbles on the pool's floor. The Grih were too light-boned to do this, she had discovered. She had to move her arms in a churning motion to keep herself down and when she ran out of air, she rose slowly back to the surface.

Everyone was on the bank, looking at her.

"You have good lung capacity," Jia said, sounding a little breathless.

Rose slicked the hair back from her face. "It's wonderful down there. I recommend it."

It looked like there were no takers though, so she did another dive down, swimming a circuit around the pool and then joined the others for lunch in the sun.

Like it had yesterday, exhaustion suddenly squeezed her in its grip, and she lay on a thin, waterproof blanket on the ground in the sun to dry off, her eyes drooping, her body wanting nothing more than sleep.

Hri Rivel shook her shoulder to rouse her when it was time to go.

"I don't want to," she said, half-asleep. "I want to stay right here." She struggled up, blinking. She didn't want to leave, but if she was difficult, if she wasn't a team player, Kila would maybe push back against having her join the explorations team in the future, and she didn't want that. She yawned. "Sorry, I'll get moving."

"We will only go on for another hour, and return this way, so you can stay here if you want." Kila adjusted the straps of her pack. "We can leave the perimeter alarms Lieutenant Appal's people set up around the clearing while we ate lunch in case anything we haven't anticipated comes through, but I doubt anything will." She paused. "If you would reactivate your lens, you might capture more than we would have otherwise if you lie still like you were."

Now that was a plan she could get behind.

"You've got a deal." Rose smiled at Kila with a great deal more warmth than she felt earlier. "See you in an hour."

Jia looked between them. "You sure you'll be all right to stay here alone?"

Rose nodded. "It's just an hour. And you can leave the perimeter alarms."

Jia wavered, then acquiesced. "See you then. Don't wander off. Stay here."

"I promise."

They left, and Rose lay back down, enjoying the privacy, enjoying the silence.

Sweetpea chirped and then crawled up to curl into a tiny ball of fluff on her chest, and Rose fell back asleep with a smile.

CHAPTER 5

ROSE WOKE WITH A SHIVER.

The day had lost its warmth, something that confused her as she dragged herself out of sleep.

She didn't feel refreshed. She still felt tired.

She opened her eyes to find Sweetpea staring at her from her perch on Rose's chest.

"Hello, baby." Her voice came out rusty, and she sat up carefully, cupping Sweetpea with a hand to keep her from falling.

As she got her bearings, she saw the reason for the cool weather was the sun was much lower in the sky.

She frowned and tapped her earpiece. "Sazo?"

"Yes?" He sounded distracted. She hadn't spoken to him much today because she had been in the group the whole time.

"What's going on?"

"There's some strange signal activity coming from Vuyn. I'm trying to work out exactly where it's coming from."

Rose shivered, and not from the cold this time. She paused in the middle of pulling on her pants. "That's weird. We're the only ones here."

"You *should* be the only ones there, certainly."

The way he phrased it didn't make her feel any better. She sat down heavily and began pulling on her socks and boots.

Sweetpea leaped from her shoulder now she was closer to the ground, gliding a fair distance, and then hopping on something Rose guessed was another bug.

When she turned her cute little face to Rose in triumph, there was a leg and a wing sticking out both sides of her mouth.

"I don't like you being down there when I don't know who else might be down there, too." Sazo's voice suddenly sounded a lot more focused. And worried.

"This is Grihan airspace, though. Might it be an old probe or something?" There was no sense getting all worked up for no good reason.

She got back to her feet, and then it struck her. The others weren't back yet. Midday was definitely a long time ago. Way more than an hour, anyway.

She sucked in a breath. "I think something might have happened to the exploration team. They should have been back by now."

"What? Where are they?" Sazo's question was quiet. Tinged with panic.

"I wanted to rest in this clearing we stopped in, and they were only going to be another hour. They left the perimeter warning beacons activated for me, and I fell asleep. I only just woke up now and a lot longer than an hour has passed."

"They shouldn't have left you." Sazo's voice was tight with anger.

"I wanted them to, and I'm fine. It's them I'm worried about." She rolled up the blanket she'd slept on, made sure there was no trace of her presence left, and then walked around the clearing switching off the warning beacons and adding them to her pack.

"What are you doing?" Sazo asked.

"I'm going to very quietly, very carefully, go the way they did, and see what might have happened to them."

"You think the signals I'm hearing have something to do with their disappearance?"

"What do you think?" she asked.

"I think it's too much of a coincidence. And I don't want you to go."

She sighed. "It's better to know what's happening and be prepared though, right?"

He thought about it. "Yes. Be careful then. Promise."

"I promise," she said, softening her voice. "I will be sneaky as."

"Sneaky as what?" he asked.

"Sneaky as the sneakiest thing you can think of. I don't know what's particularly sneaky in Grihan airspace, but I'll be that sneaky."

He laughed, as she hoped. "That would probably be a bunin."

"I'll be sneaky as a bunin," she promised. "And when we have time, you can show me what a bunin is." She moved out of the clearing, with Sweetpea riding shotgun on her shoulder, little paws holding tight to her hair.

Grihan standard operating procedure was to mark any path taken with small blue tags attached to the trees, in case anyone got lost and needed to find their way back alone. It made following the path the team had taken extremely easy.

She walked their route for ten minutes before she found where they'd been ambushed.

The ground was churned up and a few small things lay on the ground. A nutrient bar wrapper. A piece of fabric, as if someone's clothes had been ripped. There were no more blue tags from this point forward and Kila would never, ever leave rubbish lying on the ground on a planet with a non-interference order. Never.

"We're in trouble," she whispered to Sazo as she backed away from the scene.

"What is it?" His voice was low and urgent.

"Someone's grabbed them all. And that includes Jia's team."

That would explain why the ground was so churned up and also the ripped cloth. They had put up a fight.

She stood in the growing darkness of the forest, considering her options. Sazo must have been doing the same, because he was as silent as she.

Suddenly, Sweetpea started to chirp, a long, high note of warning.

"There's someone coming." She barely breathed the words out for Sazo, and then pressed herself against the tree. Sweetpea kept up her call, getting louder and more panicked and then she leaped off Rose's shoulder onto the tree trunk, where she spread herself out so her dark brown, mottled fur made her almost completely disappear in front of Rose's eyes.

Rose realized she could reach the first branch, and something about the panic in Sweetpea's call motivated her to move. She hauled herself up, and Sweetpea jumped back on her shoulder as she climbed up to the next branch, and then the next, until at last she was above the leaf canopy.

She heard the murmur of voices only moments later.

Sweetpea let out a final, high-pitch squeak and then went silent, her little body pressed against Rose's neck.

Rose didn't understand the language spoken, so she carefully removed her earpiece and held it out in case Sazo would be able to capture some of what was said and tell her later.

Whoever was below moved to the site where everyone had been taken, but not for long. She heard the voices fade, and after what felt like a long time Sweetpea suddenly relaxed, hopped back onto the tree trunk, and blinked her enormous, cute eyes at Rose.

"Did you hear them?" she asked Sazo when she put the earpiece back in, and realized he'd been shouting at her for a while.

She winced. "Sorry. I held the earpiece out to see if you could catch the language so we could work out who they are."

"Krik." Sazo's volume was still turned up. "It was at least two Krik."

Rose frowned. "I've never met a Krik, but aren't they vassals of the Garmman? Or at least their planet is in Garmman airspace." She watched Sweetpea explore the tree trunk, although the little glider kept looking back at Rose to make sure she was still there.

"They are the Garmman's responsibility. Although the Garmman keep trying to wash their hands of them. If there's any piracy in any airspace, the Krik are often behind it. And I wouldn't be surprised if the reason the mine station sent out that distress signal was because Krik were attacking," Sazo said.

"You think they drew the *Barrist* away deliberately?" If so, Dav and the crew of the *Barrist* were walking into a trap.

"If they did, and it's likely, it was probably not to attack the *Barrist*, but to get it away from Vuyn. They know they can't take on an explorer, so they tried to distract it."

What he said made sense, and she realized he had said it to soothe her.

He wouldn't have seen the need a few months ago, but he was learning.

"They might have hoped you would go with the *Barrist*, too, Sazo." In fact, they had to have been hoping Sazo's Class 5 battleship would leave even more than the *Barrist*.

"They would have had to change their plans when I didn't," Sazo said.

"Like kidnapping the exploration team." Rose crouched down and tried to see through the leaves, but given how relaxed Sweetpea was, she had to believe there was no one waiting for her below.

"Can you use the branches to walk back to the camp without going back down to the ground?" Sazo asked.

Rose gave a snort. "No. Dara told me it was like a highway up here, but the picture I had in my head was not the reality. It probably is a highway, but for birds and little gliders like Sweetpea." The foliage and the crisscrossing branches were too dense for her to move from one tree to another. Or not without a lot of difficulty. Her idea of running along wide branches high above the ground had crumbled to dust the moment she'd seen what was up here.

"Then be careful. I'll commandeer the autopilot on the explorer. You run back to it and I'll get you out of there."

Rose was silent for a beat. "No, Sazo."

"What do you mean *no?*" He sounded genuinely confused.

"I'm not going to leave the others down here while I escape to safety. Although definitely take over the autopilot of the explorer and see if its outside lenses can see any Krik."

"I've already sent a message to Dav," Sazo said, and she could hear the serious tone in his voice. "He'll be coming back as fast as he can. It'll take at least half a day for the message to get to him, though. So it's best you're safe up here with me."

"In the meanwhile Jia, Dara, and all the others could be hurt. Aren't the Krik violent?"

"That's why I don't want you down there, Rose. They're extremely violent." Sazo sounded panicked.

"It's okay," she said to him, keeping her voice soothing. "It's hard for you to worry about me, but I can't leave the others. It's in the code."

"What code?" He didn't sound like he believed her.

"The code that you never leave your friends behind."

That silenced him.

"Like you didn't leave me behind. Or Bane?"

"Yes, like that."

He was silent a little longer. "I don't like it, Rose."

"You're going to help me. I don't think they realize they missed someone. We need to work out what they're doing down here and where they're keeping everyone prisoner."

"I can start looking now, but if they're in the forest, I won't be able to see them."

"I think I can follow the tracks they've left, but I should probably go back to camp and get whatever gear I can that might be useful."

"They may be at the camp," Sazo warned.

"I know. I'll be careful." She held her hand out for Sweetpea, who jumped onto it with a little hop, and then ran up to settle herself on Rose's shoulder.

She climbed down the tree, and as she dropped to the ground, Sweetpea must have thought they were practicing gliding because she launched from Rose's shoulder and swooped to land a little way away.

"Clever girl," Rose whispered. She crouched down and Sweetpea jumped onto her shirt.

The Krik had gone, and when she went back to the spot where the team had been taken, she saw they had been on clean-up duty. They had cleared the ground.

There was nothing there now, and even the churned up soil had been smoothed over.

She stared at it, heart sinking. The Krik were covering their tracks, and if they'd also smoothed over the path they'd taken, she wouldn't be able to follow it back to where they were keeping her team.

Things had just gotten harder.

CHAPTER 6

IT WAS late by the time Rose approached the camp.

The exhaustion that had gripped her at midday, and which adrenalin and fear had burned away, was back.

Vuyn's two moons lit up the sky, both of them full and bright. It made her journey easier, and she was extremely grateful again for the clearly marked path of blue tags. She would definitely have been lost without it.

It gave her hope that the Krik hadn't been this way, or surely they'd have taken the tags down.

She slowed as she spotted the tents through the trees, and stopped completely before she stepped into the clearing, listening for any hint of the Krik.

When she heard nothing, she walked quickly toward her tent, pulling out the thin mattress and the sleeping bag, and stuffing them into her pack, along with spare clothes and her food. She stepped out of the tent with regret and then walked through the camp, looking for anything she might find useful.

The teams' clothes and food were well secured and Rose left them. She couldn't carry them all and they were of no use to her.

She looked over the more sophisticated equipment which was in the tech tent and decided she didn't want it in the Krik's hands.

She moved out of the clearing, past the eco-toilet and over the stream, and found a big tree that would hide her from view. She left all her things there and went back to camp.

First, she found a ground sheet, and then hunted for a thick bush that had enough space beneath it to hide the equipment, then she carried it, piece by piece, shoving it under the leaves and branches, and when it was all in place, she found another waterproof sheet to put over it, tucking it in all around, to keep out any rain.

She had felt tired when she reached the camp, now she felt barely able to function, but the sound of voices coming toward her worked like a cattle prod on her, so she pulled it together, took a final look around the camp and then slipped away toward her things.

"Was that the Krik?" Sazo asked.

She was amazed he had been able to hear them from her earpiece. "Yes."

"Hide."

"I am." She barely whispered it.

Sweetpea was awake again, but she was silent this time, her head and big ears swiveled toward the camp no matter which direction Rose turned.

Rose hopped the stream and settled down between the roots of the tree she had chosen, curling up and putting the sleeping bag around her like a blanket.

She heard the Krik talking, but they were quiet, and the exhaustion dragged at her, making her afraid. She had never been so tired. It was debilitating.

She tried to stay awake, but even against the interests of her own safety, she felt the pull of sleep. A few hours, she thought as she made herself as comfortable as possible, and then fell head first into it.

"Rose." The shout in her ear startled her awake, and Rose jerked up, putting her hands out blindly for balance.

"Yes?" The question croaked from her throat, and she pursed dry lips.

"I was getting worried." Sazo sounded a little frantic.

Getting her bearings, Rose leaned against the tree trunk and felt a quick, hard knock of shock against her chest as she realized it was morning, and not early morning, either. She hadn't slept for a few hours, she'd slept a good eight.

A little chirp came from above her, and when Rose tipped her head back further, she saw Sweetpea looking down at her from higher up the trunk. The little glider was facing down, her tiny claws anchoring her to the bark as she gave another chirp.

"Morning, cutie." Rose kept her voice to a murmur, suddenly aware she had no idea where the Krik were, and stood slowly, stretching out the kinks a night among tree roots had put into her back.

As soon as she was standing, Sweetpea jumped to her shoulder, and Rose gave her tiny, fluffy body a gentle stroke.

She bent to get some water out of her pack, and the same nausea she'd experienced the day before slammed into her again. She put a hand out to balance against the tree and lowered her head, and after a moment it passed.

This planet was doing a number on her.

"So, what can you tell me?" she asked Sazo as she sipped the water, and rummaged through her pack for something quick and easy to eat.

"I received a message from Dav, which must have been sent before he received mine, that says the Krik have taken the mining station hostage, and are threatening to kill everyone unless they get some supplies from the *Barrist*. While they were negotiating, the Krik seeded the airspace around the *Barrist* with mines, and have shot at every small craft the *Barrist* has sent out to try and clear them."

"They're trying to trap them there." Rose chewed on a nutrient bar.

"They *have* trapped them there. Dav wants to keep the miners safe, so he'll negotiate with the Krik as long as he believes they are going to keep their word about not harming anyone if they get what they want." Sazo's tone was neutral.

"You think that's a mistake?" Rose asked.

"I think those miners might already be dead. The Krik get caught up in their violence sometimes. Oris said Paxe showed him visual comms of them getting out of control."

And Paxe, Sazo's fellow Class 5 brother, would know, Rose thought. He'd used the Krik for his own purposes before he'd self-destructed, and had nearly killed her friend Imogen in the process.

"I'm sure Dav will ask for proof of life." But what could he do if they refused, other than go ahead on the hope that the miners and their families were still alive?

"I have other news, too." Sazo sounded grim, now, and Rose felt a chill run through her.

"Bad news, by the sounds of it."

"Yes." Sazo had been angry when they'd first met and helped each other escape the Tecran, but she hadn't heard that particular tone from him in a long time. "The Krik have surrounded the explorer craft. You couldn't come back to it and get up to me, even if you did want to."

Rose blew out a breath. She should have anticipated that. Of course the Krik would look for the ship the exploration team had arrived on. It was the obvious thing for them to do. "Good thing I don't want to do that, though. Although it would be good to have a clear shot at getting back to it after we free everyone and try to leave."

That was pretty optimistic, even for her. She couldn't even keep her eyes open, let alone work out a way to find the team and rescue them.

"I've obviously instituted the defense protocol, so when they get close enough to the small defense cannons, I shoot them." There was something darkly satisfied in Sazo's voice. "I got two straight away, which sent them into a frenzy, so then I got three more when they threw themselves at the explorer. Eventually they worked out the perimeter, and most of them have left. There are only two there now, standing guard."

"Is that because they don't have enough people to do whatever it is they're doing down here?" Rose wondered. "Maybe they can't spare the people to keep watch on the team, and guard the explorer."

"Rose." Sazo sounded hesitant. "The team might not—"

"Might not what?" She was a little sharper than she meant to be.

"You know what." Sazo's voice was as gentle as she'd ever heard it.

"The team *are* alive, Sazo. I can't believe the Krik would kill them all. I'm going to find them now."

"Please don't. Just stay hidden and wait for Dav to come. Please. Or I can send a drone to an open clearing and give you the directions to it. Then you can fly up." There was a desperation in Sazo's voice that really sliced her deep, and lit a spark of fear in her, too.

For her, she had no doubt, he would burn worlds to the ground.

She needed to deal with this before she did anything else.

She sat beside her pack, watching Sweetpea grab seriously large ant-type insects as they marched over one of the tree roots and pop them into her mouth like grapes or M&Ms. "Sazo, I don't want to frighten you, or make you worry. All I can do is tell you that I would do the same for you—I *have* done the same for you, and for Bane— and I will be as careful as I can. I don't want to get caught any more than you do, but I can't just leave the team down here and flee to safety. You can help me by scanning the forest and seeing if there is anything that looks out of place or wrong. Look for trees that have been cleared, any sign of a spacecraft. Also try to decode those signals you were picking up yesterday. Whatever can give us an idea of what's going on." Maybe having something to focus on would help him.

He was silent for a moment. "This is because you want them to like you more than they do, isn't it?"

She closed her eyes for a moment, and took a deep breath. "Maybe a little bit. But even if they didn't like me, and I knew they never would, I would still try to help them, because the Grih are my people now, and I wouldn't just walk away and let them suffer if I could help it."

"What would Sherlock Holmes do?" he asked.

Wow. They hadn't talked about Sherlock Holmes for months. She'd thought he'd forgotten about it.

"Sherlock would be applying his mind to the reason why the Krik are here. That's the key to understanding what is happening. They wanted the *Barrist* and you gone. Was that because they were expecting a spaceship to arrive and didn't want it intercepted or caught? Or is the spaceship already hidden in the forest somewhere, and they need to clear the airspace so they can get off the planet with whatever it is they have stolen from it?"

"I listened in to what the Krik who surrounded the explorer said before they attacked it, and they seemed worried about a collection." Sazo sounded more like the calmer, friendlier version of himself that he'd become.

"Keep listening to the guards for more information. Maybe even play with them. Didn't you once pretend to be a Tecran over the comms system to bring Dav and Filavantri Dimitara over to your ship so that you could trick them into bringing me my handheld?"

"I did." Sazo sounded thoughtful. "I'll have to be careful with how I do it, because if they work it out . . ."

"They'll stop talking. But it will also make them nervous about anything they hear over their comms, so either way, you hinder them," she said.

He hummed in agreement, and Rose put out her hand for Sweetpea to jump onto. She had obviously eaten her fill of ants and was just watching them now.

"I'm going to look for the team. I'll tell you what's happening when I think it's safe, but otherwise, I'll be as quiet as possible."

"Just be careful, Rose." Sazo's voice was soft. "I don't know what I'd do if you were hurt or killed."

"I will be careful." Because if she wasn't, she didn't know what he'd do, either.

CHAPTER 7

IN THE END, it wasn't hard to find them.

Rose just had to follow the sound of a spacecraft engine.

It had cut out by the time she'd reached it, but the initial roar had given her the direction to go in.

Now she lay on a branch high in the trees and looked down at the hive of activity below.

The Krik were unlike anything she'd ever seen. Their hair was a shock of pearlescent white, standing up in shaggy abundance, and their skin was a pale peach. They were slim, around the same height as her, but she could see the definition of their muscles through their shirts, both the men and the women. Twice, when someone accidentally bumped someone else as they loaded the spacecraft parked in the clearing, teeth had been bared, to reveal long, sharp incisors.

The spacecraft was a little bigger than the explorer, but not by much, and a lot older. Old Garmman tech, perhaps.

It was parked in a clearing that wasn't naturally occurring but had been created by hand. The reason Sazo hadn't seen it, though, was the camouflage net that covered most of the open space. It must look like part of the forest from above.

The Krik were coming and going from the spacecraft into the

mouth of a cave, which was set into a hill. They disappeared into the darkness and then returned with boxes that seemed too light to hold anything much. Unless the Krik were much stronger than they looked and she was wrong about the weight of what they carried.

The exploration team sat on the ground to one side of the cave mouth. None of them seemed to be restrained, but then perhaps the Krik didn't have enough restraints to go around. Chances were they'd been taken completely by surprise by the arrival of the *Barrist*.

Kila, Dara, Jia and the others were huddled together, surrounded by perimeter warning beacons, set much closer together than usual, and two bored looking guards stood on either side of them, shockguns held against their chests.

Some of the team looked injured, including Jia, and Rose saw Hri Rivel was tending to a soldier lying on the ground.

Sweetpea chirped beside her, and Rose kissed the top of her little head.

She needed to get a message to them and let Jia know she was here, watching and waiting for a chance to help them escape.

Rose crawled back along the branch to the tree trunk, where she'd left her pack. She dug through it for her notebook, a real one she'd found in Sazo's stores. She'd started writing in it most days—a journal of her new life.

She didn't dare write anything on the piece of paper she tore out, she was too afraid of it getting into the Krik's hands, but maybe just the sight of the paper itself would be enough to let the team know she had come for them.

She folded it carefully into a tiny paper airplane, and wondered if it would even make it as far as the group.

She couldn't get any closer than she was now, so it would have to.

She left her pack against the trunk and then crawled back out along the branch. Sweetpea chirped as she hitched a ride on Rose's back, as if she was having fun, and even though the circumstances weren't great, Rose smiled.

When she was as far along the branch as she could go without worrying about it snapping, Rose lifted the smaller twigs out of the way to get a clear line of sight to the others, aimed the airplane at Jia, and threw it.

She held the twigs back so she could see if it made it, but almost the moment the airplane left her hand, Sweetpea gave a chirp of delight and leaped after it, gliding way better than the paper, which she snatched out of the air.

The flutter of paper, the movement of Sweetpea's jump, had Dara turning her head, and Rose saw her eyes widen as Sweetpea landed on the ground near them, the edge of the paper airplane in her mouth.

One of the Krik guard's turned to look as well, and Sweetpea froze, big eyes staring at him.

She let go of the paper, and a gentle breeze lifted it away. Sweetpea gave a squeak of outrage at the loss. She turned away from the guard and pounced on the paper again.

As soon as she had it, she held it in her mouth and ran straight back to the tree, disappearing from Rose's view.

The Krik guard watched her with an indolent gaze which slowly swept the tree Rose was lying in.

Rose realized she was still holding back the twigs. If she could see the guard, it was possible he could see her.

She carefully let go in increments, gently letting the leaves fall back in place.

When there was no shout of surprise, she assumed she had managed to get away with not drawing the guard's attention.

She lay still, waiting for Sweetpea to come back, and thought about what she'd seen below.

Beside the guards watching over the exploration team, there weren't any others patrolling or keeping guard that she could see. The Krik obviously thought they were secure.

They were moving fast, dumping the boxes in their spacecraft and running back into the cave for more, and she wondered if this was an acceleration of their plan because Sazo continued to sit, all deadly prickles, over their heads.

After what felt like a long time there was a little chirp behind her, and then the light weight of Sweetpea running along her back.

The little glider jumped into her cupped palm, paper plane still in her mouth, and Rose stroked her, then almost snorted out a laugh as the baby curled up and went to sleep, the paper clutched in one little paw.

All tired out after that big adventure.

She had certainly helped to let the team know they were here.

Rose reversed back to her pack for some water and another nutrient bar, and pondered what to do next.

"I need a distraction. Can you give me one, Sazo?" she asked softly.

"I could shoot them," Sazo offered.

Rose thought about it. "Shoot them, where?"

"Shoot their spacecraft."

"Can you see it?" She didn't think he could.

"I can send down a drone, scan for it."

That made sense. "Only if you can be accurate. The team are near the spacecraft, and so am I."

It was his turn to pause. "I'll see. I've already launched the drone. I can also scout for a clearing where I could land the drone for you to use as an escape if things don't work out the way you plan."

She could see the sense in that. "That sounds good."

"The drone will be down in about ten minutes." Sazo said. For the first time since the Krik had taken the team, he sounded more himself.

Rose decided it was better she was away from the clearing when Sazo's drone buzzed the Krik, so she put the sleeping Sweetpea into the top of her pack and climbed down, moving back to the camp she'd set up the night before.

She heard the drone come overhead.

"I see the clearing," Sazo said. "The camouflage net is very good, but it can't fool a low-level scan."

"What's their reaction?" Rose asked.

"Panicked." Sazo sounded amused. "They've sped up their loading, although it looks as if the spacecraft is nearly full, anyway."

"What's happening with the team?" she asked.

"The team—" Sazo suddenly went quiet.

"What is it?" Rose didn't like that silence. Not at all.

"They've dragged Dara into the middle of the clearing, and they're pointing a shockgun at her head." Sazo spoke softly, and she heard the drone turn away from the clearing and head upward.

"And now?"

"Wait. I seeded a small lens into the trees as the drone left. Give it a moment to find a spot with a good angle of the whole clearing."

She waited, bottom lip caught in her teeth, on her feet in agitation.

"They've hit Dara. I don't know why—the drone was gone, and they don't seem to suspect there's a lens on them." Sazo sounded astonished.

"They were taking out their fear and anger on her." Rose's hands fisted.

"I . . . can understand that. I did that, when I got free of the Tecran." Sazo's voice was thoughtful. "I don't think the soldiers I killed were innocent, like Dara is, but they weren't personally responsible for my situation, and I killed them anyway."

This was a moment of real self-reflection for him, Rose knew. But there was no time to ponder it now.

"We can talk about that when this is over. Can you see if Dara's all right?"

"She's unconscious," Sazo said. "Dr. Revil is tending to her, and Kila is standing in front of her, between her and the Krik, now that she's back in the group." Sazo paused for a moment. "The guards are moving the group into the caves, now. Some of Jia's people are carrying Dara and one other person in, and the lens can't pick them up anymore."

"And the Krik?"

"They've all come out the cave and they're closing up the space-craft. Some of them are starting a fire in a fire pit. They look like they're settling in for a while."

"What could they be waiting for?"

"Me to leave?" Sazo asked.

"Maybe." She thought about it. "Is there somewhere you can hide?"

"What good would that do? They're bound to be suspicious of it. After all, they saw my drone, and they know we know they have the team."

"True." It was too late now to change the game. "I think they took the team initially not as hostages, but to round them up and keep them from interfering in whatever they're doing. You didn't go with the *Barrist*, and you sent down the drone when the team went missing, so they know it's no use being secretive anymore. Their only hope is to use the team as a bargaining chip. A way to get off-planet."

"So do we let them do that?" Sazo asked.

"We could." If it would mean the team were safe, she didn't care what the Krik were doing. They could figure out what they'd been up to when they had everyone back. "The best thing to do is whatever will bring everyone back, as unharmed as possible."

"Negotiating with them could take a while, and every moment they're in that cave, Dara and whoever else was injured isn't getting help," Sazo said.

"I agree." She didn't want them in the Krik's clutches for a moment longer than necessary.

"Rose." Sazo's voice sounded a little odd.

"Yes?"

"I have Dav coming through the comms, he's within hailing range."

She slid down onto the ground. "The *Barrist* is back?"

"No." Sazo sounded as shocked as she was. "He had Borji create a distraction at the mining station, and he snuck away in a maintenance pod, which is why it's taken him so long to let us know he's on the way. The Krik have deployed a comms disruptor at the station, and the maintenance pod doesn't have a good range."

"Can you patch me through?" she asked.

"Rose!" Dav's voice was slightly garbled, but clear enough.

"What's going on?" She didn't understand why he'd leave his ship and risk getting hit by the Krik in the maintenance pod, or being captured.

"I got Sazo's message that you were under attack by the Krik. I needed to come, but the Krik at the station seeded the airspace with mines and then they managed to get a comms disruptor going. I left Borji in charge, waiting for fleet backup, because Sazo relayed the situation to Battle Center for us earlier. A battleship will be light jumping to get here by tomorrow sometime."

"They could have taken you. Or shot you." She was shocked at the wobble in her voice.

"I was careful." His voice gentled. "I wasn't going to risk getting caught, because the whole point was to come get you."

She tipped her head back to stop tears flowing, and took a deep breath. "Thank you," she whispered. "But I'm fine. It's the team who are in trouble."

"Sazo told me. He's sending out a drone to tow my pod, so I'll reach him faster, and I'll grab some weapons from his store for us, and some supplies, and take the drone down to meet you. Don't do anything until I get there."

"I can't promise that," Rose said. "If the Krik start hurting the team and there's something I can do about it, I will. But otherwise, I'll keep away. Sazo has a lens in the tree outside the cave they're in, so we know what's happening."

"I promise I'll be as fast as I can. Sazo will find a good place to land the drone, and will tell you where to meet me."

She suddenly had the sense Dav and Sazo were managing her.

"You'll tell me if the Krik start hurting the team again, Sazo." She didn't make it a question, but she knew it was.

"If there is something you can do about it," Sazo said.

She could tell a carefully parsed sentence when she heard one. "You two are ganging up on me, aren't you?" She yawned, and felt guilty about it. It was only afternoon and the team were in danger. She had no business wanting to sleep.

"We want to keep you safe. If there is something you can do to help the others, I'm sure Sazo will tell you," Dav said. There was something almost irritatingly soothing about his tone.

She was too tired to argue about it. If there was nothing she could do right now, she'd better try to get some sleep and get up her energy to fight them both later. "Okay."

There was a moment of silence.

"Rose, are you all right?" Dav's voice went from soothing to sharp.

"Just tired. You try sleeping in amongst tree roots with Krik prowling around you."

"She's been nauseous, too," Sazo said, helpfully.

"I'm fine." She mumbled it.

"I'll be down soon, Rose." Dav's voice crackled, and broke up, and after a long moment of silence, Rose guessed the connection had been lost. "How long 'til he gets to you?" she asked Sazo.

"Five hours maximum. I'll put out the weapons and supplies I think he'll need and have them ready for him, so he should be down shortly after that. And I'll look for a good clearing to land the drone in."

"Okay. I'll just rest for a bit." She had taken out her pillow and sleeping bag as she talked, and she got comfortable. She thought Sazo might have said something in the affirmative to that, but she was already half asleep, and then sleep took her under.

CHAPTER 8

DAV JALLAN HAD TRIED to sleep while Sazo's drone towed him back to Vuyn, but worry kept him from being able to get any real rest.

Worry for his crew on the *Barrist* was one thing, although hopefully that was just a waiting game, with Borji drawing out negotiations with the Krik to give Battle Center a chance to send help.

As drawing things out seemed to suit the Krik's purposes, too, that shouldn't be a problem, but then, so far, nothing had gone according to plan, so why would things start now?

Worry for Rose and his explorations team was something else all together. They were in immediate danger and Rose hadn't sounded herself.

Sazo had confirmed his impression, telling him she seemed unusually tired and had had several bouts of nausea.

"She says she's been too long in space. That she needed to be down on the planet more than she realized," Sazo told him. "So I'm doing something about that."

Dav wondered what he could possibly be doing other than finding planets for her to visit, but he had too much on his mind to ask.

Sazo's drone pulled him through the Class 5's gel wall, and he had grabbed his gear and was out of the maintenance pod before it had even come to a stop.

He stopped short when he saw the array of weapons laid out on the floor, and the stack of supplies. "You're organized," he said to Sazo.

"I wanted to save you some time."

Dav had no illusions that Sazo wanted to help him in any way. The faster he could leave on the drone, the sooner Rose would have some help, and that's all Sazo cared about.

That was fine with him, though. He could look after himself. It helped to know Sazo always had Rose's back.

He picked through the weapons, choosing some because they would be easy for Rose to use as well, and others because Sazo let him play around with the weapons the Tecran had accumulated from all over the galaxy occasionally and Dav had wanted a chance to try them out in a real situation.

"I've put the food Rose likes to eat in that box," Sazo said, and a hovering drone touched the one he meant.

Dav knew that meant it was specially for Rose, and no one else had better touch it.

He grinned. "Got it. And the rest?"

"Food that the Grih like," Sazo said, almost grudgingly, as if he didn't want Dav to think he'd gotten soft, just because he'd thought of Dav and the team's comfort.

"Thanks. I'm ready to go."

"Good." Sazo was obviously as eager for Dav to get below as Dav was, which suited them both fine.

Dav hoped there was never a time when what he wanted for Rose and what Sazo wanted diverged, because Sazo was a fearsome enemy to have, and he was in Rose's life to stay.

While he considered that, four hover drones descended and packed the larger drone. While they were busy, he got into his tactical gear, so he was ready for anything once he reached Vuyn.

"You've found a good place to land?" he asked as he tucked his helmet under his arm and started toward the drone.

"It's not ideal, because it's some distance from the Krik's position, as well as the explorer, which they're still guarding, but it'll be safe enough for you to land there and get your things out before the Krik can get to you. I'll bring the drone into orbit once you're out, ready to drop down if you need it as a means of escape."

Dav nodded. That sounded like the best option, given what they had to work with.

He climbed in and Sazo didn't waste any time shooting the drone out of the flight deck and down toward Vuyn.

Rose had been so excited to go down here, and it had turned into a nightmare.

The United Council would have to do something about the Krik. They had been putting it off for years, trying to force the Garmman to do the right thing and get control, given the Krik's planet was in Garmann airspace, but enough was enough.

They needed to be slapped down, and hard, for this.

Dav thought about the weapons Sazo had loaded into the drone's hold, and didn't feel even the slightest pause at the thought of using them.

Rose picked her way carefully through the trees toward the drone's landing site.

Sazo had woken her an hour before the drone landed, to give her time to find the way, and she had splashed some water on her face to wake herself up, eaten an energy bar and left her things in the tree's roots again, just taking a small pack.

It was pitch dark, around midnight, and Sweetpea seemed to think they were going on a great adventure.

Rose wondered if she wasn't nocturnal.

She hadn't seen any other gliders, not once, but that could be because they were living their cute little lives overhead, above the leaf canopy.

"You'd have died if I'd left you there, Sweetpea, but I don't want to deprive you of a happy, natural life, either."

Sweetpea turned her head to look at her and chirped and Rose couldn't help kissing the top of her furry head. Sweetpea reached up and patted her cheek with a paw and Rose knew it would be very, very hard to leave her behind when the time came.

She cuddled her close to her chest and picked her way through the trees, hoping she'd understood Sazo correctly on the direction.

"You should hear the drone any moment," Sazo said.

Just as he spoke, she did hear it, the hum growing louder.

It came in with no lights, Sazo in control of piloting it the whole way, and Rose heard the swirl of leaves up ahead as it touched down.

She started to jog as fast as she could, suddenly desperate to see Dav.

Sweetpea chirped in excitement when she sped up, and then they were in the clearing, with Dav already stepping out of the drone's narrow door. He was wearing his battle gear, which made him look even bigger than he was.

He saw her and jumped down to the ground and she flew into his arms.

He lifted her up and then gave a grunt of surprise when Sweetpea chirped.

"What the—?"

"I made a friend," Rose said, and swallowed hard because she was weepy again. She held Sweetpea to the side and went on tiptoe to kiss Dav.

He pulled her close and the kiss turned from desperate to something hotter and edgier.

She pulled back when a bird started a *kak kak kak* from the trees, and Dav traced her cheeks with his fingers.

"What's this, tears?" His voice was soft, and the gentleness of it tipped her over the edge and she started weeping in earnest.

"Rose, what's wrong?"

She could hear the panic in his voice, and it helped center her. She gurgled out a laugh.

"Nothing, I'm really fine. Just feeling everything a little more than usual. I think it's being down on the ground."

Sweetpea made a strange squeak, and then ran up her arm and leaned forward, putting her paws against Dav's collarbone.

"A very little friend," Dav said, giving her head a stroke.

Sweetpea chirped again and jumped onto his shoulder, turned and jumped back onto Rose's.

"Let's get everything out of the drone so Sazo can send it into orbit." Dav turned and activated a small hover drone, which floated out, and then loaded it with three large packs.

"That hover's pretty quiet, but it's not silent," Rose said.

"We need to find a spot to set up camp and then we can turn it off."

Rose saw it was big enough to carry a person, and she caught the implication immediately. They may need it to transport someone on the team who was too injured to walk.

"I've got a spot, which is close to where they're holding the team, but it's at least a forty minute walk from here. Equidistant from the caves and where the explorer craft is."

"Sounds like as good a spot as any." Dav slid an arm around her, pulled her close, and nuzzled her hair. "I was worried. It's very good to see you're fine."

She nodded. "I was worried, too. I didn't think it was a good idea for you to leave the *Barrist* in a little maintenance pod, but it's so good to see you, I'm not going to give you a hard time about it."

He chuckled. "I'm glad to hear it."

She held his hand as she showed him the way through the trees.

The birds above were making far more noise now than they had been when she'd come through earlier, so she guessed the low hum of the hover was disturbing them. Hopefully their calls would drown out any noise the hover made.

Sweetpea was fascinated by the hover and kept jumping from it to Rose and back again.

Rose hadn't dared to use the blue tags to mark the way, in case a Krik stumbled upon her path, so she had to stop a few times to orientate herself and it was over an hour before they arrived at her tree.

"Good spot." Dav unloaded the hover and switched it off, and the sudden silence was almost deafening.

Sweetpea leaped back onto the hover and stared over at Rose in surprise that it was now silent and unmoving, and Dav chuckled.

"She's cute."

"Too cute. I'm already deeply in love."

"Kila giving you a hard time about it?" Dav asked.

Rose sent him a grin. "Funny how you guessed that straight off."

He gave a snort. "You can handle Kila."

That was true. She could.

Feeling suddenly better about everything, Rose pulled him into a hug, kissed his cheek, and then stepped back, hands on hips to survey the bags he'd brought.

"What's all this?"

"These are the weapons Sazo put together for me, and the other two are supplies. One box for you, the other for the rest of us." She could hear the humor in his voice.

"Sazo did that, too, I assume?"

Dav's only answer was a soft laugh.

He never minded that Sazo put her first in everything. It was something she found hard to get used to, but Dav approved. It was how he and Sazo had come to an accommodation with each other.

She was glad they had, but she wished they would find common ground in areas other than just herself. One day, maybe they would.

Dav began to pull items out of the weapons box into a bag, and leaving him to it, Rose went to look in the supply boxes.

"*Edventa!*" She slapped a hand over her mouth in surprise at the noise she'd just made. "Sorry," she whispered. "But just, yay!"

"You are happy," Sazo said.

"Sazo, you are an absolute legend. Seriously, a million brownie points to you for sending down some *edventa* for me. I love you."

"I know you do. That's why I sent it down." He spoke formally, but Rose knew he absorbed her declarations of love like a hot desert sand in a rain shower. He needed it. He hadn't heard anything positive for the first years of his life.

Rose found her hand was shaking when she tried to open the pack of *edventa*, the hailstone shaped chocolates which the Tecran had stolen from a planet in the far-flung galaxy. Sazo had been able to reproduce them, and it was as close to chocolate as it was possible to get.

"You aren't okay." Dav took the pack from her, opened it.

"I think I'm hungry and I've been so busy and worried, I just haven't realized it," she told him. "I've got the shakes and I think that's low sugar levels. I just need to eat a bit more and I'll be fine."

Dav looked at her skeptically. "Sazo says you've been exhausted and nauseous as well."

She shrugged. "I have, but I don't feel sick now, and it's not like I'm . . ." She trailed off, and stared at him in utter shock. She slowly put a hand to her stomach. "Hri Rivel said it could take months before she'd know if there was a chance we could—" She swallowed hard. "Dav. I might be pregnant."

It was his turn to look at her in shock.

She had had an IUD which would have been due to be replaced if she'd stayed on Earth, so she'd had Hri Rivel remove it, and she and Dav had decided they were fine with the consequences of not using birth control while Hri and other Grihan doctors worked on what to them was a fascinating problem of finding out what Grihan birth control solutions would work for her, and if it was even possible for her and Dav to conceive.

That had been less than a month ago.

"Just so I understand. You're saying . . .?" His gaze went to where her hand rested on her stomach.

She nodded, and was suddenly in his arms.

"This is good news. This is the best news I've ever had." He held her gently, and then set her down. "You have to go back to Sazo, now, Rose. No question."

"What news?" Sazo asked.

"I think I'm pregnant. I'm going to have a baby."

Sazo considered her declaration in silence. "You are happy?"

"I'm very happy. And you will have another friend."

She saw Dav's quick look of worry, and gave a tiny shake of her head.

How she dealt with this now would set the tone. Sazo could be a terrible, deadly enemy, or he could be the most powerful, faithful friend her child would ever have.

Dav's reserve was the result of the cultural issues the Grih had with artificial intelligence—thinking systems, the Grih called them.

But Sazo and his fellow Class 5 brothers were part of Grihan reality, now.

"That's why you've been feeling off?" Sazo asked.

"Sometimes at the beginning of a pregnancy, women get really tired and feel a bit nauseous. It even explains why I've been so weepy."

"Sazo, I want Rose to get in the drone and come back to you." Dav said.

"I agree, but the drone's just gone into orbit. It'll be two hours before I can get it back into position to come through the atmosphere and land in the same spot."

Dav swore softly.

"I'm pregnant," Rose reminded him. "Not ill."

He shot her a cautious look and then grinned. "I know. But I want you safe."

"I want you safe just as much, and you aren't even pregnant."

"Fair enough." He turned serious. "But the Krik are not gentle and the thought of you in their hands for any reason . . ." He shook his head in a sharp, hard movement. "No."

She didn't like the idea either, but she also didn't like the idea of being sidelined simply because she was pregnant.

A wave of exhaustion suddenly hit her and she yawned. "How about this? I show you to the cave and you can watch what's happening there for a bit. I'll wait for you back here, and then we can walk back to the drone when it lands together."

"That works." He tilted his head in that Grihan way of his. "But we'll need to be careful, because the Krik will have heard the drone land the first time and might just be checking out where it landed." He picked up the weapons he'd taken out of the bag and she nodded, then yawned again. Sweetpea had curled up on the hover and gone to sleep, and Rose left her there rather than disturb her.

Dav insisted she pick a weapon, and she chose one she'd been interested in since Sazo showed it to her a while ago, a slim t-shaped device that fitted nicely in her palm, so the stem of the *t* poked between her fingers and the bar sat snugly in her hand.

It was meant to restrain, and it did so with frightening efficiency. You didn't need to aim if you didn't want to, you could simply slash the air in front of you and a thin fibre of light—some kind of filament—shot out and hardened as it hit the air before coiling around whatever was in front of it.

The best part was it was coded for the user, so if the Krik took it off her, they wouldn't be able to use it on her or anyone else.

She felt her heart hitch a little, because every other option in the bag was lethal—clearly neither Dav nor Sazo were feeling particularly forgiving—and she guessed they had included this one because they knew she would hesitate to use something more deadly.

As she led Dav down the by now familiar path to the caves from her tree, she contemplated the idea of motherhood.

She liked it. A lot.

She would have preferred to have been more settled in Grihan society, have more of a network around her, but she still had nine months to achieve that.

It wasn't impossible.

Dav was as quiet as she was, mainly, she knew, because of the danger of the Krik, but he had to be reeling from her news, as well.

It was a big day for them both.

"Are you happy?" she whispered as she reached the tree she'd used before to spy on the Krik.

"Yes." His response was just as quiet, and he touched his lips to her ear. "I'm very happy. And excited. And scared."

She smiled, turning her face against his neck to nod. "Same."

"I'll walk you back," he offered and she shook her head.

"I could stay with you."

He shook his head.

They stared at each other, neither wanting to let the other go, and then they both smiled.

"I bet we look pretty sappy right now," she said.

He grinned. "I don't care how we look."

She lifted her face and he kissed her, and finally, she walked away.

He didn't move, watching her leave, and only when she looked over her shoulder at him did he sling his bag of strange weapons over his shoulder and start to climb.

CHAPTER 9

ROSE KNEW something was wrong when she heard Sweetpea making the same high-pitched cry she'd made when they'd hidden from the Krik the day before.

She didn't know why she immediately thought the baby was up against a natural predator, something from the local fauna, but when the Krik stepped out and aimed a weapon at her, she was genuinely shocked.

"Krik," she said, for Sazo's benefit. Her thoughts went straight to her own weapon, sitting in her pants pocket, but the Krik could easily shoot her before she could pull it out.

"Like you didn't already know." The Krik holding the shockgun opened his mouth in a show of incisors.

"How did you find me?" she asked.

"One of the guards on watch was walking back to the caves and heard a noise. Probably this hover here. He called us and we came looking for it."

Damn.

"Who else is here that we missed?" the Krik asked.

"No one. That's why the Class 5 above sent down the hover. I couldn't carry these supplies by myself." Thank goodness Dav had taken the bag full of weapons.

"Delivered by that drone from earlier?"

Rose nodded.

"Why didn't you get out of here, to safety?"

"I don't leave my friends." Rose shrugged.

"Well, come join them, then." He motioned with the shockgun, and as he did, Sweetpea leaped from the tree trunk, where she'd taken refuge, onto Rose's shoulder, and hissed at the Krik.

The Krik hissed back, and Sweetpea ducked under Rose's hair. She could feel her shivering.

"I've seen some of those in the trees, but none of them are that friendly." The Krik looked at her suspiciously.

"I rescued this one. She's a baby."

He looked skeptical, but she moved in the direction he pointed without hesitation, and from behind her, she heard the hover start up.

When she glanced back, two Krik she hadn't seen earlier were walking next to it, and one flashed his incisors at her when he caught her looking.

Dav was going to be so mad.

Not that this was her fault, but still . . .

Exactly what he feared had just happened.

"Ask them how much value they put on their spacecraft," Sazo said in her ear. He was cold as ice.

She wondered why he'd taken so long to react to her telling him about the Krik, but knowing him, he'd have been working out all his options.

"Do you think that's a wise move?" she asked him.

"They need to feel some consequences. They got their way with Dara, and they think they've got the upper hand. We need to teach them they do not."

"You think this isn't wise?" the Krik asked.

"I wasn't talking to you," Rose answered. "The Class 5 wants to know how much you value your spacecraft."

The Krik grabbed her shoulder so fast she couldn't help the squeak of surprise that came out of her. His mouth was open, his incisors bared. "Is that a threat?"

"Tell them it's a promise," Sazo said.

"He says it's a promise."

The Krik stopped dead, his hand digging into her shoulder. "What exactly is he promising?"

"Um, to destroy your spacecraft unless you let me go," Rose said.

The Krik tightened his grip until Rose cried out in pain, and then he looked surprised, as if he hadn't even realized what he was doing. He held on for another moment, just to let her know he could hurt her, and then released her. "Why didn't he make that same threat for the others?"

"He was still considering his options before now." She rubbed her shoulder. She wouldn't tell him Sazo didn't have the same attachment to the others.

"Who is he, anyway? The captain?"

She blinked. Did they not realize Sazo *was* the Class 5? "Yes, he's the captain."

"Tell him if he backs away and lets us leave, we'll leave you and the others down here. We'll leave a timed explosive with you, and when he lets us out of range, he can fetch you all. If something happens to us before then, you go *boom*."

"He's lying," Sazo said. "They don't have a timed explosive with them. I've scanned their ship. Which means he's probably lying about leaving you down here, or leaving you alive."

"I agree." Rose narrowed her eyes at the Krik. "He doesn't believe you."

The Krik shrugged. "Take it or leave it."

Sudden laser fire shot down from above, and the Krik reacted like a scalded cat, spinning to face the caves, and letting out a screech.

Rose said nothing, although she was tempted to say it looked like Sazo intended to leave it.

The Krik rounded on her, and she lifted up both hands. "I didn't do that."

"Tell him if he does it again, you die." He shoved her and she stumbled back, only just able to keep her footing.

"Tell him, if you die, then I will have nothing stopping me from destroying everything." Sazo's voice was low. "The spacecraft, the caves, and whoever is coming to fetch whatever it is they've loaded into their hold."

Rose swallowed.

"What did he say?" The Krik grabbed the front of her jacket and shook her, and she batted at him, sick of being manhandled.

She jerked out of his hold and clenched her fists. "He says if you kill me, there will be nothing stopping him from destroying every-thing. You, your ship, your caves and whoever is coming to fetch whatever's in those boxes in your spacecraft's hold." She took a breath and spoke the stone cold truth. "Your very existence depends on keeping me unharmed."

Of course, it was probably too late for that now. Just the threat to her life would have done it, let alone the pushing and shoving.

These Krik were dead men walking.

She just needed to be sure she was walking too, by the end of it.

"There are other hostages in the caves, we don't just have you." The Krik said it slowly, like remembering a get-out-of-jail-free card.

"I'm afraid they're a bit more expendable, where he's concerned," Rose said with an apologetic shrug.

The Krik turned to respond, but before he could speak they heard shouts and other noise, and the spacecraft engine started up.

"Sounds like your spacecraft is fine, so it was just a warning shot," Rose said, and the Krik grabbed her upper arm and pulled her the last few steps into the clearing.

Rose risked a quick look at her tree, and made a face she hoped Dav could see. Sweetpea had been hiding under her hair for most of the walk, but now she emerged onto Rose's shoulder, and looked at the tree, too.

The Krik who was holding her arm called out in his own language, and there was a lively back-and-forth with another Krik standing beside the spacecraft.

The ground next to it was scorched.

Sazo had been absolutely accurate with his shooting.

She would expect nothing less.

Whatever had been discussed, some of it must have been an order to put her in the cave with the others, and she was dragged over to the entrance.

As she was pulled along, the night lit up as a second shot came down, this time on the other side of the ship.

With a cry, Sweetpea leaped from her shoulder, and Rose tried to turn to see which way she went, but the Krik's hold on her tightened.

"Tell him to stop." The order was screamed at her.

"Stop restraining me, let me go, and he will." She pulled her arm out from under his grasp.

"You're our way out." The Krik shoved her, and she landed on the ground in the entrance to the cave.

"Are you all right?" Sazo asked, and his voice was tightly controlled.

"I'm fine," she murmured.

"How many Krik are in the cave with you?"

She knew if she said none, he would light up the spacecraft like New Year's Eve fireworks and Dav could take his chances in the firestorm. "Four."

The device in her pocket suddenly became a lot more comforting.

"Dav?" she asked Sazo as one of the four Krik guards dragged her deeper into the cave.

"He's unhappy," Sazo said, and there was a dry humor to his voice, sort of a self-deprecating tone, that made her think he was mellowing a bit. Taking himself less seriously. Realizing he and Dav shared a few things.

It was better than the icy calm from earlier.

"I bet." She struggled to her feet, dusting the back of her pants with her hands, and looking around. "I . . ."

She shuddered, and something of what she was feeling must have come out in her voice.

"What is it?" Sazo's tone had sharpened.

"Spiders." She was not a squeamish person, but this many spiders was enough to freak anyone out. "Lots of spiders."

"Move." The Krik guarding the cave shoved her toward the back, and she followed a wide path that had been cleared of webs, although she saw above her head new webs were already being spun.

The members of the exploration team were penned in against a cave wall, surrounded by a waist-high wall of crates like ones the Krik had been carrying to their spacecraft.

"Rose." Jia Appal rubbed at her hair in frustration at the sight of her. "Was that Sazo shooting?"

"Yes."

The guard pointed to the small gap between the boxes, and Rose slid through.

"Hey, you don't look Grih," he said, as she stepped into the light the Krik had set up to shine into the little corral they'd created for their prisoners.

"Yes, I am," Rose said. "What else would I be?"

He studied her for a moment, and then shrugged. "Your ears are wrong," he told her, and then walked away.

"There's nothing wrong with my ears," Rose muttered, almost amused at herself with how indignant she felt. She suddenly wondered if her and Dav's child would have pointy ears like him, or round ones like hers.

It set off another sudden round of emotion, and she had to close her eyes to compose herself.

"Rose, are you all right? Did the fuckers hurt you?" Kila asked, worried.

"I'm okay. They just shoved me around a bit." She straightened her jacket and then slipped her hands into her pockets, and closed her right hand over her weapon. "Sazo is threatening to blow up their spacecraft if they hurt us."

Jia raised a brow at the 'us', but didn't contradict her.

"Rose." Dav's voice was suddenly in her ear. Sazo must have set up a relay for him. She waited for him to say something else, but her name was obviously weighty enough.

"It wasn't my fault," she said. "They were waiting for me when I got back to the tree. They heard the hover."

Jia watched her quizzically as she spoke.

"Dav," Rose mouthed. "He's not happy."

"He's here?" she mouthed back.

She nodded.

"Are the others in the cave with you?" Dav asked, and she had the sense he was trying to put his emotions aside and be practical.

"Yes. Everyone's here, and there are four Krik guarding us." She spoke with her back to the guards, as if she was having a quiet conversation with Jia. "This place is full of spiders."

"Tell Dav they're similar to hyr spiders," Kila said. "But their silk seems to have a couple of different properties. I don't know how the Krik discovered them, but they've been harvesting the silk and packing it up to be transported out."

"I heard that." Dav sounded thoughtful. "Sazo thinks they're waiting for their buyer, and that's why they tried to lure us away."

"Would be interesting to see who that buyer is, wouldn't it?" Rose asked.

"Very interesting," Sazo agreed.

Because whoever it was was knowingly doing a deal with the Krik on a non-interference planet in the middle of Grihan airspace. That was worth a bit of investigation.

"So what's the plan?" Jia asked.

"Sazo wants to blow them all up, Dav wants to kill them all, and I've got the means to restrain them." Rose flashed her device at Jia. She shook her head when the lieutenant held out her hand to take it. "Coded to me, sorry."

"Ah, one of the strange ones Dav tells me Sazo has in his stores?"

She nodded. "It's pretty efficient."

"That's fine with me. Anything that gives us the upper hand." Jia looked over at one of her team—Wester, it looked like—and Rose saw he was still lying down, and he didn't look well.

"Dara?" she asked, suddenly panicked that she couldn't see her friend, but then Kila moved and Rose saw she'd been blocking Dara from the Krik's view.

Her problems with the explorations officer melted away at the sight of her protectiveness of her people. She should let go of her grudge, and try again with Kila.

Dara was also lying down, but she seemed more awake than Wester.

"Two of the team are seriously injured," she said, and hoped Sazo was relaying it to Dav. "The others are either only slightly injured or fine. Oh, and the Krik obviously have our supplies and the hover."

There may have been a time delay, or Dav was silent for a long time.

"I'm very tired of these Krik."

She heard something implacable in his voice.

"I agree," Sazo said. "And what do you know, the buyer for their silk just came into range. And their system isn't encrypted with Paxe's encryption key."

Which meant Sazo would soon be in control of their ship.

"What's happening?" Jia Appal mouthed to her.

"The Krik's buyer just arrived. Sazo's tracking him," Rose whispered. "Dav, have you seen Sweetpea? She ran toward the tree you're in when Sazo took that second shot."

"She's here," he said. "Staring at me with those big eyes from the end of the branch."

"Thank you," she whispered. "We'll get out of this."

"Yes, we will." The implacability was still in his voice. "Can you take the guards?"

"I'll talk to Jia. But yes, I think I can." She knew this could end badly for the guards. She could even kill them if the restraints caught them around the neck, and she couldn't keep the nerves and the squeamishness from her voice.

"They will kill you, Rose. They won't think twice about it."

"I know. I'll let you know when we're going to move." She turned to Jia. "We need to come up with a plan to neutralize the guards. My weapon can restrain them."

"That's fine with me." Jia gave a smile that had Rose blinking.

It spoke of retribution and blood.

"How does it work?" Jia asked as Rose pulled it out of her pocket again.

"It creates a very fine, strong filament that wraps around things and restrains them." Rose's hand crept to her stomach and she pressed her palm against her shirt. Her resolve hardened.

She looked over at the guards. They had ranged themselves across the cave entrance, looking outward as if waiting for the next hit from Sazo. Occasionally one turned to check on them, but not often enough to be safe. She wondered why they weren't more vigilant, and said so to Jia.

"Perimeter warnings," Jia said, and pointed, and Rose finally noticed the perimeter beacons they had been using outside were now set up around the half-circle of crates.

"My weapon's range is at least to the cave entrance, so we won't set off anything until the guards are down."

Jia motioned Kila over. "What you're saying is you can take the guards, but then the warning beacons will go off as we escape, and the Krik outside will come straight for us?"

"They'll try to come straight for you, but I will make it very difficult for them," Dav said, and Rose started. She hadn't realized he was listening in.

"And so will I." Sazo sounded like he was starting to enjoy himself. "The buyer turns out to be a Garmman trader who got permission to enter Grihan airspace on the pretext of needing to go to Larga Ways. He's been neutralized."

Rose hoped Sazo meant that he'd taken over the Garmman's systems and had put the trader into a holding orbit, not that he'd switched off the environmental systems on the ship and was killing everyone on board. He'd chosen to do both in the past, and she didn't have the time to ask which one he'd decided to use this time.

"Dav and Sazo say they'll open fire as soon as the guards are down, so hopefully no one will be headed for us, and if anyone does come our way, I still have my device," Rose said.

"And me and some of my team will have those four guards' weapons," Jia said, with a smile that was not in the least bit nice.

Jia and Kila turned away casually, and moved through the group, letting everyone know what was about to happen. Rose was glad to see three of Jia's team and one of Kila's moved to Wester and Dara, standing beside them, ready to pick them up and run.

The other three in Jia's team began to move to the edges of the waist-high wall of crates, ready to jump over.

Rose got a good grip on her weapon and moved to the narrow opening in the corral. The device always fought to go upward, the energy powering it so strong it lifted in her hand whenever she'd used it in the practice range on the Class 5. To counter that, she clamped her left hand over her right wrist to help keep it steady and straight, and then she switched it on.

It came alive with a hum, the sound eager to Rose's ear. And a little bit sentient.

She let it lift up her hand until she was pointing it at the ground but her hands were chest height, and then she slashed quickly from right to left, drawing a figure of eight in the air, which lit up with the glow of the thin red filament.

For a moment it seemed as though nothing had happened.

Jia glanced at her, questioningly, and then all four guards fell over. They shouted in surprise at being tied together. The restraints seemed to be made of cooling silver wire that was either still hot, or sharp enough to cut into them, because she could see they were bleeding where the wire bound them. By the time they hit the ground, they were screaming in rage and pain.

Jia whispered a long, drawn out curse of surprise. "I want one."

The four helpers lifted their two injured team mates and Rose ran out of the enclosure.

Before she was more than a few steps out, Jia and her team were alongside her, and the perimeter warning began to blare.

Jia and the three others scooped up the guards' weapons, wincing at the noise the beacons were making, and in a move so practiced it must have been part of their training, they hit all four guards with the butt of their shockguns, rendering them unconscious.

Rose stopped just past them, looking out into the clearing.

"We're out and the four guards are taken care of."

She had barely finished speaking before the spacecraft rose straight up and disappeared.

"Was that you?" she asked Sazo into the sudden, stunned silence.

"I found a way in to their system using the comms they had with the Garmman trader. I didn't want to risk any debris hitting you or Dav if I hit them with a laser strike."

"Nice work."

Except now, the other Krik in the clearing all turned toward them, toward the blare of the perimeter warnings. There were only ten at most, but there was murder in their eyes.

As they started to run toward them, Jia and her people opened up with shockgun fire. The Krik faltered in the face of it, lifting their own shockguns, and Rose looked wildly around for cover.

She could survive a shockgun blast, but she was sure it wouldn't be good for her pregnancy.

Suddenly, to her right, a blue glow blossomed. It expanded almost in slow motion, and as it reached the Krik, it lifted them off their feet and threw them across the clearing, as if a giant beast had swiped them away with a claw.

For a moment, there was absolute silence as everyone tried to work out what had happened.

A scream of rage came from above her, and Rose spun and looked upward, just in time to see a Krik leaping from the slope above the cave entrance down onto them.

He landed between her and the mouth of the cave, out of Dav's line of sight, and bared his incisors as he lifted his shockgun.

She wouldn't have time to activate her device and use it before he shot, Rose realized, even as she lifted it up.

Out of nowhere, and with a screech of rage, a little furry handkerchief with big eyes sailed through the air, landed on the Krik's head, screeched again, and then leaped at Rose.

The Krik shrieked in panic, lifting both hands to his head to work out what had landed there, and as soon as Sweetpea was on her shoulder, Rose flicked the device and watched the Krik fall sideways as the filaments went from glowing red to silver, wrapping around his raised arms, his waist, and his upper thighs to his knees.

She switched it off and stuck it in her pocket, and then lifted Sweetpea off her shoulder to cuddle her close under her chin and give her little head lots of kisses.

"Such a good girl. So brave and clever." She didn't realize she'd switched to English until some of the Grih turned in her direction, a look on their faces that she knew meant they were fascinated and entranced by the sing-song rhythm of her words.

Everyone straightened a little, turning to look in the same direction, and she saw Dav emerge from the trees. He'd been in his tactical gear the first time they'd met, and this moment reminded her of that, when he'd rescued her from an enraged gryak, a sort of bear-like creature, and opened up a whole new world of possibilities for her.

"What weapon was *that*?" Jia asked him and he murmured something as he walked past her, handing her the weapon in his arms.

He kept going though, not stopping until he was standing in front of her.

He pulled off his helmet and set it on the ground, and she reached out, cupping his elbows with her hands and tilting her face to look up at him.

"Nice shooting."

He stared down at her, no humor on his face, not even in his eyes.

"I don't want that to happen again," he said.

"Me, neither," she smiled up at him. "But life happens."

He narrowed his eyes at her. "Rose."

"How likely is it to happen again?" she asked.

"Not likely. I'm going to make sure they do something about the Krik. They're ambitious, they want to increase their standing in the United Council, but their ambition has gone too far here."

"Great." She stepped a little closer. "And now that we've sorted them out down here, can we stay and finish the job we came to do?"

He looked like he wanted to say no, but didn't want to deny her anything, either.

"No reason not to stay," Kila said, coming up to them. "Especially now we have these spiders to study. If this is a type of hyr silk, which I think it is, this could be a way for us to make our own, instead of depending on the current supply."

Dav sighed. "We're down here, now, I suppose. But I might have to get back to the *Barrist*."

"Borji is bringing the *Barrist* back," Sazo said. "I sent him the decryption key to the Krik's systems, and he was able to neutralize them at the mining station. They've got a few wounded miners in the medbay, and Sub-lieutenant Nur has secured the Krik, and will wait for you to come back and fetch him and his team on the mining station."

"Sounds like everything is in hand," Rose said.

Dav shook his head as she grinned up at him. "Sounds like."

He pulled her close, under his arm.

Around them, Jia's team were securing the Krik, and Sweetpea had been watching them with bright-eyed interest, but she suddenly leaped onto Rose's head.

When she landed back on Rose's shoulder, she had a spider in her paws.

"Was that in my hair?" Rose looked at it in horror as Sweetpea took a delicate bite of it. "That's a very good girl," she praised, and Sweetpea finished the spider off and then tucked herself under Rose's chin.

"You all right?" Dav asked, and there was a lot packed into that question.

Rose tightened her grip on his waist. "I really am."

CHAPTER 10

"I DON'T KNOW what to do." Rose knew she was being indecisive, which was really unlike her, but she was in a quandary of her own making.

Sweetpea did not want to go her own way.

Rose had left her on a tree and walked away a few times now, and with a chirp of distress, the little glider had raced after her and needed a lot of cuddles to calm down again.

At the same time, Rose didn't like life onboard a spaceship. Why would Sweetpea?

"Look at it this way," Dav said, and she could hear the hint of exasperation at the situation in his voice. "She would be dead without you. She doesn't want to leave you and you don't want to leave her. Just take her with you."

Sweetpea gave a chirp of agreement.

"What if she's unhappy onboard?" Rose was so torn, and she hated it.

"Then Sazo can bring her back. I'm sure he wouldn't mind."

"Dav's right," Sazo said. "We can bring her back anytime. And you would like coming back, too, wouldn't you?"

Rose sighed. She knew she was already considered a special case amongst the Grih. She, Fiona Russell, Imogen Peters and Lucy Harris were the exotic new additions to the Grih population, and having Class 5s run errands for her was only going to make her stand out all the more. But what the hell, she did want to come back here, and if Sweetpea got sick of space, then they'd bring her back and let her be happy here.

"Thank you. Let's do that."

Dav made a sound she interpreted as the Grih version of *thank God*, and she couldn't help the snort that escaped.

"I was being difficult, wasn't I?"

Dav turned to her and rubbed a thumb over her cheek. "You can be as difficult as you like."

She outright laughed at that.

"It's good to hear you laugh. I don't think you've done much of that for a while now. I want you to be happy."

"I'm happy, I promise. I was just missing nature around me. We can make a point of going down to more planets, now that the Tecran problem is over."

He gave a nod of agreement. "We can."

"Ready to come up now?" Sazo asked, and she thought there was an eagerness in his voice she hadn't heard before.

"Sure. Let's go." She put Sweetpea onto her shoulder and walked up the explorer's ramp.

Kila glanced up at her from her seat, took note of Sweetpea on her shoulder, and gave a nod.

So either Dav had spoken to her, or she understood.

Either way, it looked like she wasn't going to give Rose a hard time about it.

Sweetpea was intrigued by the interior of the explorer, and she kept everyone onboard amused with her chirps of excitement and her leaps from shoulder to shoulder as she explored.

When the explorer slid through a gel wall, Rose was surprised to find they'd come straight to Sazo.

"We'll get off here," Dav told her. "The others will go back to the *Barrist*."

They were the last of the team to go up. Everyone onboard the *Barrist* had had a chance to come down and have a break on Vuyn while they searched the forest for signs of what the Krik had been up to. They'd found more than one camp, and evidence of mineral sampling as well as a second spider cave that looked as if it had already been harvested, although the spiders were starting to reestablish themselves.

Rose said her goodbyes to the team and stepped off with Dav. He would go over later to take over from Borji, but she was glad they had a few hours to themselves.

Since they'd told Hri Rivel they were pretty sure she was pregnant, the doctor wanted her to come over for a full medical checkup, and she didn't want to put that off too long.

Little hovers appeared to whisk away their things and Sweetpea grabbed hold of her hair as she took in the flight deck.

"I hope you're happy here, little one," Rose said, giving her tiny head a stroke.

"I have a surprise for you," Sazo said.

"A surprise?" she glanced at Dav, but he shrugged.

"Go through the doors, and you'll see it."

Rose walked to the flight deck double doors and they opened silently as she approached them.

The smell from Vuyn below, of green and growing things, hit her, and she took a deep breath in as she blinked in surprise.

What had once been a passageway with a wall across from the flight deck doors was now a walkway with a railing.

Sazo's Class 5 was built like a spiky ball, and it was as if the center of the ball had been scooped out.

She stepped up to the railing and looked down, and gasped.

Dav came to stand beside her, hand on her shoulder, as she looked down at the explosion of green below.

"You've made a garden." She could barely get the words out.

"There are only two of you on this ship, and it was built for five hundred. I decided we could use some of the space for other things, so I rearranged the interior." Sazo sounded suddenly hesitant. "Do you like it?"

She started to sob, hands coming up to cover her face as she shuddered with the emotion of it. "I love it. I cannot say how much I love it," she managed to get out. "How did you get the plants so big so quickly?"

Sazo started to tell her, something about growth hormone and something in the water, but she stopped listening to him and started walking toward the tube to get down below to see for herself.

Dav had said nothing so far, but he kept pace with her.

"Did you know about this?" she asked as she wiped tears away with the back of her hand.

"Sazo told me he was doing something to help you feel more at home in space, but I didn't know what exactly he was planning." He looked introspective.

"What is it?" she asked as the tube whisked them down.

"I should have seen it myself. How unhappy you were. But I didn't."

"I didn't know how much I missed being in nature until I was on Vuyn," she said, taking his hand. "We've been busy avoiding a full-out war, remember. We've only just got clear of all that."

He gave a slow nod, but she could see he wasn't convinced.

The tube opened up directly onto a pathway that wound through raised flowerbeds and mature trees, and Rose realized she'd have to get Sazo to explain to her again how he did it, because it was amazing.

With a happy chirp, Sweetpea jumped off her shoulder onto a tree and disappeared into the leaves, and something that had still been knotted inside her loosened.

Sweetpea could be happy here. Just like her.

She turned to Dav, and leaned into him, and as his arms came around her, she lifted a hand, touched it to her lips, and blew a kiss in the direction of the nearest lens to say thank you to Sazo.

Things would be just fine.

Other books in the Class 5 series:

DARK HORSE (BOOK 1)

Some secrets carry the weight of the world.

Rose McKenzie may be far from Earth with no way back, but she's made a powerful ally--a fellow prisoner with whom she's formed a strong bond. Sazo's an artificial intelligence. He's saved her from captivity and torture, but he's also put her in the middle of a conflict, leaving Rose with her loyalties divided.

Captain Dav Jallan doesn't know why he and his crew have stumbled across an almost legendary Class 5 battleship, but he's not going to complain. The only problem is, everyone onboard is dead, except for one strange, new alien being.

She calls herself Rose. She seems small and harmless, but less and less about her story is adding up, and Dav has a bad feeling his crew, and maybe even the four planets, are in jeopardy. The Class 5's owners, the Tecran, look set to start a war to get it back and Dav suspects Rose isn't the only alien being who survived what happened on the Class 5. And whatever else is out there is playing its own games.

In this race for the truth, he's going to have to go against his leaders and trust the dark horse.

Dark Horse is the winner of a Galaxy Award and the Prism Award for Best Futuristic 2016.

DARK DEEDS (BOOK 2)

Far from home . . .

Fiona Russell has been snatched from Earth, imprisoned and used as slave labor, but nothing about her abduction makes sense. When she's rescued by the Grih, she realizes there's a much bigger game in play than she could ever have imagined, and she's right in the middle of it.

Far from safe . . .

Battleship captain Hal Vakeri is chasing down pirates when he stumbles across a woman abducted from Earth. She's the second one the Grih have found in two months, and her presence is potentially explosive in the Grih's ongoing negotiations with their enemies, the Tecran. The Tecran and the Grih are on the cusp of war, and Fiona might just tip the balance.

Far from done . . .

Fiona has had to bide her time while she's been a prisoner, pretending to be less than she is, but when the chance comes for her to forge her own destiny in this new world, she grabs it with both hands. After all, actions speak louder than words.

DARK MINDS (BOOK 3)

The mind is the most powerful weapon of all . . .

Imogen Peters knows she's a pawn. She's been abducted from Earth, held prisoner, and abducted again. So when she gets a chance at freedom, she takes it with both hands, not realizing that doing so will turn her from pawn to kingmaker.

Captain Camlar Kalor expected to meet an Earth woman on his current mission, he just thought he'd be meeting her on Larga Ways, under the protection of his Battle Center colleague. Instead, he and Imogen are thrown together as prisoners in the hold of a Class 5 battleship. When he works out she's not the woman who sparked his mission, but another abductee, Cam realizes his investigation just got a lot more complicated, and the nations of the United Council just took a step closer to war.

Imogen's out of her depth in this crazy mind game playing out all around her, and she begins to understand her actions will have a massive impact on all the players. But she's good at mind games. She's been playing them since she was abducted. Guess they should have left her minding her own business back on Earth...

DARK MATTERS (BOOK 4)

DARK MATTERS . . . taking matters into her own hands

A time bomb, waiting to go off . . .

Lucy Harris is on the run, not sure where she can turn to for help, or if help is even available. But even as her abductors chase her down, she realizes they don't just want to recapture her, they want to erase her.

When your very existence puts a planet at the risk of war, there's no choice but to do everything in your power to stay out of your enemies hands.

A predator . . . waiting for the chance to pounce

The powerful AI battleship, Bane, is accompanying the United Council envoy to Tecra to mete out the punishment the Tecrans have earned for breaking UC law. He revels in the power he's about to have over his old masters. But his mission isn't only to rain down retribution on the people who kept him chained for years, he's also looking for a human woman his fellow Class 5 mentioned in the final seconds of his life. Paxe admitted to taking Lucy Harris from Earth, and Bane has been looking for her ever since.

A warrior conflicted . . .

Commander Dray Helvan thinks the Grih made a mistake in not pushing for war with the Tecran, but he's had to accept the compromise, that he and the other envoys from the United Council will go to Tecra and dismantle its military from the top down. His mission is not one of his choosing, but when he and his team arrive, he's handed a very different job. While he distrusts Bane on principle, when the thinking system tells him there's a woman running for her life on the planet below, he will do whatever he has to to see her safe. And if that means war for Tecra, well, then it means war.

DARK AMBITIONS (A CLASS 5 NOVELLA)

Rose McKenzie is adapting to life with the Grih, and now that the threat of war with the Tecran is over, she's hoping to settle into what passes for a normal life far from Earth and everything she knows. When she gets the chance to join an exploration team who are going down to collect information from a planet in Grihan airspace, she jumps at the chance to stretch her legs and breath some real air.

But unknown to the Grih, someone is already on the planet, and they don't want anyone to know what they're up to. They ambush the exploration team and take them prisoner, but they don't realize they didn't get everyone. They didn't get Rose.

With her lover, Dav, and his spaceship the *Barrist* lured away by a distress signal, Rose and Sazo, along with a furry friend Rose has made, are the exploration team's only hope at rescue.

Note: DARK AMBITIONS is a novella set in the Class 5 series world and occurs after the events in DARK MATTERS, book 4 in the series.

DARK CLASS (BOOK 5)

Waking up alone . . . Ellie Masters comes out of a coma to find herself the only inhabitant of an eerily empty moon station. She's not on Earth any more, she's not even in the right solar system. So when someone reaches out to her, tells her he's her friend, she's happy to believe it. The alternative is to be stuck alone with an enemy.

The hunt of his career . . . Grih Battle Center captain, Renn Sorvihn, has been chasing a rogue Tecran ship for over a month, convinced its captain is simply trying to delay his inevitable surrender and punishment. But when Renn follows the Tecran ship into an unchartered sector, and realises the Tecran have been working their way to a secret moon base for weeks, he suddenly understands things are most definitely not as they seem.

Caught in the crossfire . . . When the Tecran arrive, with the Grih hot on their heels, Ellie finds herself the catalyst for heightened danger to everyone. The Tecran see her as evidence of their military's crimes, the Grih see her as a massive diplomatic complication, and her presence brings the whole confrontation up several thousand notches.

But Ellie isn't alone, and her new friend has ways to help her. Time to outclass them all . . .

COLLISION COURSE: BOOK 6

A step into the unknown . . .

Rose is looking forward to meeting the Fisone as part of the United Council's outreach mission. Since the Tecran were defeated and the full scope of their crimes were uncovered, the UC has wanted to find the Tecran's victims and extend the hand of friendship. The fact that Rose is close to having her baby is just another element to the adventure of finding the Fisone's planet and seeing if they could be potential allies.

An explorer's dream . . .

Dav Jallan has been captain of the *Barrist* for a few years, but this is the first time he's headed for a planet inhabited by advanced sentients. The Fisone exist—that is indisputable—and every part of this mission is why he became an explorer in the first place. The goal is to find them, form alliances, and make friends. The fact that he's about to become a new father simply adds to his sense of excitement.

A collision course with reality . . .

When Sazo's Class 5 and the *Barrist* enter the Fisone's airspace, what they find is far from the uncomplicated meeting they had envisioned. The Fisone are divided, carrying a grudge, and are sure the Grih are no different from the Tecran they encountered the year before. When they take Rose as a hostage, both Dav and Sazo focus everything they have on finding her, and as the Fisone's actions create more and more danger, ideas of alliances, friendship, and cooperation become less and less important.

The only comfort both Dav and Sazo have to draw from is that Rose has been taken by others before, underestimated before, and her abductors have lived to regret it.

They are counting on history repeating itself.

ALSO BY MICHELLE DIENER

SCIENCE FICTION NOVELS

Verdant String series:

Interference & Insurgency Box Set

Breakaway

Breakeven

Trailblazer

High Flyer

Wave Rider

Peace Maker

Enthraller

Sky Raiders series:

Intended (Short Story Prequel Available Free to Newsletter Subscribers)

Sky Raiders

Calling the Change

Shadow Warrior

Class 5 series:

Dark Horse

Dark Deeds

Dark Minds

Dark Matters

Dark Ambitions: A Class 5 Novella

Dark Class

Collision Course

FANTASY NOVELS BY MICHELLE DIENER

The Rising Wave series:

The Rising Wave (Prequel novella to THE TURNCOAT KING and now included as bonus material in The Turncoat King)

The Turncoat King

The Threadbare Queen

Fate's Arrow

Truth's Blade

Truth's Blade Bonus Short Story (Available free to newsletter subscribers)

Mistress of the Wind

The Dark Forest series:

The Golden Apple

The Silver Pear

HISTORICAL FICTION NOVELS

Traffic Warden Mysteries:

Ticket Out

Return Ticket (Coming soon)

Susanna Horenbout series:

In a Treacherous Court

Dangerous Sanctuary (A short story - available for free, exclusively to readers who sign up to Michelle Diener's New Release Notification List)

Keeper of the King's Secrets

In Defense of the Queen

Regency London series:

The Emperor's Conspiracy

Banquet of Lies

A Dangerous Madness

Other historical novels:

Daughter of the Sky

SHORT PARANORMAL FICTION

Breaking Out: Part I (Short story)

Breaking Out: Part II (Novella)

To receive notification when a new book is released, and to receive exclusive copies of numerous novellas and a free audio book, sign up at michellediener.com.

ABOUT THE AUTHOR

Michelle Diener is an award winning author of historical fiction, science fiction and fantasy romance.

Michelle was born in London and currently lives in Australia with her husband and children.

You can contact Michelle through her website or sign up to receive notification when she has a new book out on her New Release Notification page.

Connect with Michelle
www.michellediener.com

ACKNOWLEDGMENTS

A huge thank you to Edie and Jo, who always help make my stories the best they can be. Also a huge thank you to Creative Paramita for the amazing cover.